SUSAN SCARLETT
SALLY-ANN

SUSAN Scarlett is a pseudonym of the author Noel Streatfeild (1895-1986). She was born in Sussex, England, the second of five surviving children of William Champion Streatfeild, later the Bishop of Lewes, and Janet Venn. As a child she showed an interest in acting, and upon reaching adulthood sought a career in theatre, which she pursued for ten years, in addition to modelling. Her familiarity with the stage was the basis for many of her popular books.

Her first children's book was *Ballet Shoes* (1936), which launched a successful career writing for children. In addition to children's books and memoirs, she also wrote fiction for adults, including romantic novels under the name 'Susan Scarlett'. The twelve Susan Scarlett novels are now republished by Dean Street Press.

Noel Streatfeild was appointed an Officer of the Order of the British Empire (OBE) in 1983.

ADULT FICTION BY NOEL STREATFEILD

As Noel Streatfeild

The Whicharts (1931)

Parson's Nine (1932)

Tops and Bottoms (1933)

A Shepherdess of Sheep (1934)

It Pays to be Good (1936)

Caroline England (1937)

Luke (1939)

The Winter is Past (1940)

I Ordered a Table for Six (1942)

Myra Carroll (1944)

Saplings (1945)

Grass in Piccadilly (1947)

Mothering Sunday (1950)

Aunt Clara (1952)

Judith (1956)

The Silent Speaker (1961)

As Susan Scarlett
(All available from Dean Street Press)

Clothes-Pegs (1939)

Sally-Ann (1939)

Peter and Paul (1940)

Ten Way Street (1940)

The Man in the Dark (1940)

Babbacombe's (1941)

Under the Rainbow (1942)

Summer Pudding (1943)

Murder While You Work (1944)

Poppies for England (1948)

Pirouette (1948)

Love in a Mist (1951)

SUSAN SCARLETT

SALLY-ANN

With an introduction
by Elizabeth Crawford

DEAN STREET PRESS

A Furrowed Middlebrow Book
FM86

Published by Dean Street Press 2022

Copyright © 1939 The Estate of Noel Streatfeild

Introduction copyright © 2022 Elizabeth Crawford

All Rights Reserved

The right of Noel Streatfeild to be identified as the Author of the Work
has been asserted by her estate in accordance with the Copyright,
Designs and Patents Act 1988.

First published in 1939 by Hodder & Stoughton

Cover by DSP

ISBN 978 1 915393 10 4

www.deanstreetpress.co.uk

Introduction

When reviewing *Clothes-Pegs*, Susan Scarlett's first novel, the *Nottingham Journal* (4 April 1939) praised the 'clean, clear atmosphere carefully produced by a writer who shows a rich experience in her writing and a charm which should make this first effort in the realm of the novel the forerunner of other attractive works'. Other reviewers, however, appeared alert to the fact that *Clothes-Pegs* was not the work of a tyro novelist but one whom *The Hastings & St Leonards Observer* (4 February 1939) described as 'already well-known', while explaining that this 'bright, clear, generous work', was 'her first novel of this type'. It is possible that the reviewer for this paper had some knowledge of the true identity of the author for, under her real name, Noel Streatfeild had, as the daughter of the one-time vicar of St Peter's Church in St Leonards, featured in its pages on a number of occasions.

By the time she was reincarnated as 'Susan Scarlett', Noel Streatfeild (1897-1986) had published six novels for adults and three for children, one of which had recently won the prestigious Carnegie Medal. Under her own name she continued publishing for another 40 years, while Susan Scarlett had a briefer existence, never acknowledged by her only begetter. Having found the story easy to write, Noel Streatfeild had thought little of *Ballet Shoes*, her acclaimed first novel for children, and, similarly, may have felt Susan Scarlett too facile a writer with whom to be identified. For Susan Scarlett's stories were, as the *Daily Telegraph* (24 February 1939) wrote of *Clothes-Pegs*, 'definitely unreal, delightfully impossible'. They were fairy tales, with realistic backgrounds, categorised as perfect 'reading for Black-out nights' for the 'lady of the house' (*Aberdeen Press and Journal*, 16 October 1939). As Susan Scarlett, Noel Streatfeild was able to offer daydreams to her readers, exploiting her varied experiences and interests to create, as her publisher advertised, 'light, bright, brilliant present-day romances'.

Noel Streatfeild was the second of the four surviving children of parents who had inherited upper-middle class values and expectations without, on a clergy salary, the financial means of realising them. Rebellious and extrovert, in her childhood and youth she had found many aspects of vicarage life unappealing, resenting both the restrictions thought necessary to ensure that a vicar's daughter behaved in a manner appropriate to the family's status, and the genteel impecuniousness and unworldliness that deprived her of, in particular, the finer clothes she craved. Her lack of scholarly application had unfitted her for any suitable occupation, but, after the end of the First World War, during which she spent time as a volunteer nurse and as a munition worker, she did persuade her parents to let her realise her dream of becoming an actress. Her stage career, which lasted ten years, was not totally unsuccessful but, as she was to describe on *Desert Island Discs*, it was while passing the Great Barrier Reef on her return from an Australian theatrical tour that she decided she had little future as an actress and would, instead, become a writer. A necessary sense of discipline having been instilled in her by life both in the vicarage and on the stage, she set to work and in 1931 produced *The Whicharts*, a creditable first novel.

By 1937 Noel was turning her thoughts towards Hollywood, with the hope of gaining work as a scriptwriter, and sometime that year, before setting sail for what proved to be a short, unfruitful trip, she entered, as 'Susan Scarlett', into a contract with the publishing firm of Hodder and Stoughton. The advance of £50 she received, against a novel entitled *Peter and Paul*, may even have helped finance her visit. However, the Hodder costing ledger makes clear that this novel was not delivered when expected, so that in January 1939 it was with *Clothes-Pegs* that Susan Scarlett made her debut. For both this and *Peter and Paul* (January 1940) Noel drew on her experience of occasional employment as a model in a fashion house, work for which, as she later explained, tall, thin actresses were much in demand in the 1920s.

Both *Clothes-Pegs* and *Peter and Paul* have as their settings Mayfair modiste establishments (Hanover Square and Bruton Street respectively), while the second Susan Scarlett novel, *Sally-Ann* (October 1939) is set in a beauty salon in nearby Dover Street. Noel was clearly familiar with establishments such as this, having, under her stage name 'Noelle Sonning', been photographed to advertise in *The Sphere* (22 November 1924) the skills of M. Emile of Conduit Street who had 'strongly waved and fluffed her hair to give a "bobbed" effect'. *Sally-Ann* and *Clothes-Pegs* both feature a lovely, young, lower-class 'Cinderella', who, despite living with her family in, respectively, Chelsea (the rougher part) and suburban 'Coulsden' (by which may, or may not, be meant Coulsdon in the Croydon area, south of London), meets, through her Mayfair employment, an upper-class 'Prince Charming'. The theme is varied in *Peter and Paul* for, in this case, twins Pauline and Petronella are, in the words of the reviewer in the *Birmingham Gazette* (5 February 1940), 'launched into the world with jobs in a London fashion shop after a childhood hedged, as it were, by the vicarage privet'. As we have seen, the trajectory from staid vicarage to glamorous Mayfair, with, for one twin, a further move onwards to Hollywood, was to have been the subject of Susan Scarlett's debut, but perhaps it was felt that her initial readership might more readily identify with a heroine who began the journey to a fairy-tale destiny from an address such as '110 Mercia Lane, Coulsden'.

As the privations of war began to take effect, Susan Scarlett ensured that her readers were supplied with ample and loving descriptions of the worldly goods that were becoming all but unobtainable. The novels revel in all forms of dress, from underwear, 'sheer triple ninon step-ins, cut on the cross, so that they fitted like a glove' (*Clothes-Pegs*), through daywear, 'The frock was blue. The colour of hare-bells. Made of some silk and wool material. It had perfect cut.' (*Peter and Paul*), to costumes, such as 'a brocaded evening coat; it was almost military in cut, with squared shoulders and a little tailored collar, very tailored at the waist, where it went in to flare out to the floor' (*Sally-Ann*), suitable to wear while dining at the Berkeley or the Ivy, establishments to which her heroines – and her readers – were introduced. Such details and the satisfying plots, in which innocent loveliness triumphs against the machinations of Society beauties, did indeed prove popular. Initial print runs of 2000 or 2500 soon sold out and reprints and cheaper editions were ordered. For instance, by the time it went out of print at the end of 1943, *Clothes-Pegs* had sold a total of 13,500 copies, providing welcome royalties for Noel and a definite profit for Hodder.

Susan Scarlett novels appeared in quick succession, particularly in the early years of the war, promoted to readers as a brand; 'You enjoyed *Clothes-Pegs*. You will love Susan Scarlett's *Sally-Ann*', ran an advertisement in the *Observer* (5 November 1939). Both *Sally-Ann* and a fourth novel, *Ten Way Street* (1940), published barely five months after *Peter and Paul*, reached a hitherto untapped audience, each being serialised daily in the *Dundee Courier*. It is thought that others of the twelve Susan Scarlett novels appeared as serials in women's magazines, but it has proved possible to identify only one, her eleventh, *Pirouette*, which appeared, lusciously illustrated, in *Woman* in January and February 1948, some months before its book publication. In this novel, trailed as 'An enthralling story – set against the glittering fairyland background of the ballet', Susan Scarlett benefited from Noel Streatfeild's knowledge of the world of dance, while giving her post-war readers a young heroine who chose a husband over a promising career. For, common to most of the Susan Scarlett novels is the fact that the central figure is, before falling into the arms of her 'Prince Charming', a worker, whether, as we have seen, a Mayfair mannequin or beauty specialist, or a children's nanny, 'trained' in *Ten Way Street*, or, as in *Under the Rainbow* (1942), the untrained minder of vicarage orphans; in *The Man in the Dark* (1941) a paid companion to a blinded motor car racer; in *Babbacombe's* (1941) a department store assistant; in *Murder While You Work* (1944) a munition worker; in *Poppies for England* (1948) a member of a concert party; or, in *Pirouette*, a ballet dancer. There are only two exceptions, the first being the heroine of *Summer Pudding* (1943) who, bombed out of the London office in which she worked, has been forced to retreat to an archetypal southern English village. The other is *Love in a Mist* (1951), the final Susan Scarlett novel, in which, with the zeitgeist returning women to hearth and home, the central character is a housewife and mother, albeit one, an American, who, prompted by a too-earnest interest in child psychology, popular in the post-war years, attempts to cure what she perceives as her four-year-old son's neuroses with the rather radical treatment of film stardom.

Between 1938 and 1951, while writing as Susan Scarlett, Noel Streatfeild also published a dozen or so novels under her own name, some for children, some for adults. This was despite having no permanent home after 1941 when her flat was bombed, and while undertaking arduous volunteer work, both as an air raid warden close to home in Mayfair, and as a provider of tea and sympathy in an impoverished area of south-east London. Susan Scarlett certainly helped with Noel's expenses over this period, garnering, for instance, an advance of £300 for *Love in a Mist*. Although there were to be no new Susan Scarlett novels, in the 1950s Hodder reissued cheap editions of *Babbacombe's*, *Pirouette*, and *Under the Rainbow*, the 60,000 copies of the latter only finally exhausted in 1959.

During the 'Susan Scarlett' years, some of the darkest of the 20th century, the adjectives applied most commonly to her novels were 'light' and 'bright'. While immersed in a Susan Scarlett novel her readers, whether book buyers or library borrowers, were able momentarily to forget their everyday cares and suspend disbelief, for as the reviewer in the *Daily Telegraph* (8 February 1941) declared, 'Miss Scarlett has a way with her; she makes us accept the most unlikely things'.

Elizabeth Crawford

CHAPTER ONE

Burr went the alarum clock. Ann, without as much as raising one eyelash, put out her hand and switched it off. But
having done that she did not pull her hand back into bed.
Instead she picked up the clock and held it above her head.
The position was not comfortable. In no time, as experience
had taught her would happen, she got pins and needles in
her fingers. The weak-minded at that moment would have
yielded, they would have put down the clock, pulled their
arm back cosily into bed, and settled down for another ten
minutes' sleep. But not Ann. Ann did not like seven-thirty
on a February morning when there is no fire in the bedroom
any more than most girls, but she was strong-minded. Even
before the pins and needles drove her to open her eyes and
sit up, all those things she must do between now and going
to work were being tabulated.

Put on the kettle for making tea. If she did not do it,
Mum would. Light the geyser; it was such a slow old thing
she would not get a bath unless it was lit right away. As
she came up from the kitchen, knock on Mr. Bloom's door.
That was the worst of having to take in boarders. They were
always wanting something if it was only a knock on the door.

At this point the pins and needles won. Ann sat up,
grabbed her dressing gown from the end of the bed. Shoved
her feet into her waiting slippers. Walked resolutely across
the room and pulled back the curtains.

It was just about sunrise, but there was no sun to rise
that morning. Ann peering through the frost-decorated
window at the street lamp below saw sleet swirling round it.

"Ugh," she thought. "How disgusting." Then, as an afterthought, "I'll only put a little water in the first kettle and
make Mum and Dad a cup of tea quickly. No point in us all
padding around feeling cold."

On the stairs she met Nurse Wild, another of the boarders.

"Morning, dear," Nurse said cheerfully. "Nice weather for the Eskimos."

Ann nodded, and was going to pass on; then she felt ashamed. You might not like people to be too chatty at seven-thirty in the morning, but it was brave of them, especially when, like Nurse, you had nothing to look forward to all day but the whining of a rich old woman, who, according to Nurse, was lying down and dying about ten years before she need.

"Can't you wait a second?" she said. "I'm just putting on the kettle. You'll freeze if you go out with nothing in you."

Nurse hesitated.

"I shouldn't. It's a bit of a favour my having breakfast there, and I don't want to get on the wrong side of those servants. Still, it is a bit pneumonia-ish out."

They went to the kitchen.

"Wonderful woman, your mother." Nurse looked admiringly round. "Everything like a new pin. And, mind you, these old houses are a sight worse to keep nice than the new ones."

Ann put a match to the gas.

"She is a wonder. When I was little and Dad was doing well we had somebody in every day for the heavy work. But you never hear her grumble."

"I'll say you don't." Nurse unhooked some cups from the dresser. "And she wasn't brought up to it, either, was she?"

"Not exactly." Ann, hugging her dressing gown round her, unlocked the back door to take in the milk. "Ouch, it's cold. Her father was a doctor. They never had much money, but they had to have maids for the look of the thing."

Nurse sniffed as she planted each cup on its saucer.

"Don't I know? I've seen some sad things in doctor's houses. A maid opening the door, and nothing to eat on the table."

"Dad's people were like that." Ann held her hands round the kettle to warm them. "His father was a doctor, too, you know."

Nurse nodded.

"So was your father going to be, wasn't he?"

"Yes. But grandfather died before he was through training. He left no money, so Dad learned to be a chemist."

Nurse held out the teapot.

"What about a drop to heat this?"

Ann poured a little water from the kettle.

"Of course, his shop going smash isn't so long ago. Just before you came."

Nurse fetched the tea-canister.

"How many spoonfuls?"

"Five. Sometimes when I see Dad's face and I look at all those big blocks of flats I'd like to blow them up."

Nurse laughed.

"Don't do that, or you'll blow my old lady up with them. And though she's crotchety, she's my week's wages."

Ann took the teapot and made the tea.

"Sound a Bolshevik, don't I? But Dad was doing so well. There wasn't a house for miles but came to him to make their medicines up. You would think when they build these big flats they'd think of the tradesmen round about. There's no need for them to have their own shops, Dad could have been chemist to the lot."

"I know. It's a funny world. But it'll be a funnier one if I get the sack. Pour me out my cup, there's a pet."

Ann, with three cups of tea on a tray, went up to her parents' room. She stopped on the way to put her cup and turn off the geyser. She made a face at the shallowness of the water. She was a person who, if she could choose, liked to wallow in hot water, but as she admitted resignedly, wallowing was not for her, gas costs money.

Ann's parents, Alfred and Alice, were getting up. That is to say Alfred was in his dressing gown and Alice was dressed. She was at the dressing table. She smiled at the sight of the tea.

"Are you a nice thing? I was just saying to your father, my fingers are so cold I keep dropping my hairpins."

Alfred hugged his dressing gown to him. He sat down on the end of the bed, and studied his daughter over the top of his cup.

Ann's nose, like any other nose on a cold morning, was pink at the tip. Her face had the streaky look of a face that is feeling chilly. Her brown hair, though it curled naturally, had so far been left to itself and might have been dragged through a hedge. Yet in spite of these things Ann managed to look attractive. She was not lovely, not even pretty, but she had a charming figure and a face cram full of personality. Her large grey eyes were crinkled at the corners with humour. Her nose was turned up slightly at the tip in an independent way. Her mouth, if on the big side, was full of generosity. Even at eighteen she had nothing defenceless about her.

"I've given old Bloom his knock," she said, turning away. "I'm off to my bath."

Her parents said nothing for a moment after she had gone. They went on sipping their tea. Alice put down her cup. She nodded at Alfred's reflection in the glass.

"Well, life may have treated us a bit shabbily, but it's done its best to make up when it gave us Ann."

Ann lay back in her bath and drank her tea. Her mind was turning over a problem. Should she wear her brown shoes which were smart but would let in the wet, or her black which were sensible. The black won.

"No good getting a cold," she thought, as she put down her cup and began to wash. "The clodhoppers have it."

Because a little noise is heartening in a cold room, Ann sang as she dressed. She sang that she knew her Prince would come, though it was the last thing she believed that morning. She stopped in the middle of the song to laugh at herself.

"Look at you," she thought. "Your knickers and vest may keep out the cold, but they're not romantic. Better keep princes out of it."

Because the weather was so repulsive, Ann put on a thick dress. It had been given her by a cousin. It was made of yellow and brown check. It was stuff which would have made a serviceable if unbecoming coat, but was unfortunate as a frock. Ann had taken yards out of it, and shortened it, but in spite of this even her slim figure bulged. Her mother looked in at the door just as she had got it on.

"Darling! I do hate that frock. Though—"

Ann grinned.

"Don't bother to finish. You're going to say, 'I thought it was kind of your Cousin Jane to give it to you.' It wasn't kindness, it was an evil deed, for it's too good to throw away, and every time it's cold I suffer a day's purgatory looking foul in it."

"Your overall will cover it at the shop."

Ann took her mackintosh out of her cupboard.

"That's all you know. Even an overall can't hide the bulges this frock gives me." She collected her hat, gloves and bag. "All the same, if I must look a fright, today's a good day. It's the Manton wedding. Half our customers are going; they had their faces and hair done yesterday. There won't be many in today."

"Poor bride," said Alice sympathetically. "What a day for a wedding."

"And in the country." Ann followed her mother downstairs. "It's a shame. Lady Mona's so pretty. But even the prettiest bride can't look her best in this weather. Miss Briggs is going down to do her face. I hope she'll lay the make-up on extra thick so it'll hide her nose if it gets red."

Alice put a plate of porridge on the table.

"Let that be a lesson to you. When you marry, you choose the summer."

"When!" Ann gave her mother a hug. "You ought to say 'if.'"

Ann, having finished her breakfast, put on her mackintosh. Alfred had just come down. He regarded his daughter with amused sorrow. Ann caught his glance.

"I know, darling. I look terrible. But at least I'm dry and warm. Just a plain, serviceable girl." She came over and kissed him on the end of the nose. "Nobody will look at me, so don't worry." She turned to her mother. "Is Bunny awake?"

"No. Not when I came down."

Ann pulled on her gloves. Her eyes were soft but she did not mean anyone to see that. She was a little ashamed at the feeling of protectiveness which surged over her whenever she thought of her eleven-year-old brother with his weak heart. Her voice was deliberately casual.

"Tell him from me he's a lazy little hound." She blew her mother a kiss. "Goodbye! Don't let the boarders get you down."

The Maison Pertinax Hairdressing and Beauty establishment where Ann worked was in Dover Street. Ann lived in Chelsea. There was no bus or tube very near her, so she walked to the King's Road and took a bus from there. When it was fine she enjoyed the walk. When it was like today she loathed it. The moment she opened the front door sloshy sleet slapped her in the face. It lay in slippery heaps on the curb and she had to walk carefully. Fellow pedestrians hurried by with their heads down and gloomy wet faces.

"I hope, oh, how I hope," thought Ann, "this is not one of the days when the central heating went out in the night."

The staff had to arrive at The Maison Pertinax at nine o'clock. Mr. Pert, who owned the place, kept a good receptionist to see that nobody was late. Besides the receptionist there was a staff of ten. Six hairdressers, two manicurists who could do hairdressing in a rush and two beauty specialists, Miss Briggs and Ann.

Mr. Pert had inherited the business from his father, Thomas Pert. Old Thomas had worked up a business which in the parlance of his day was strictly confined to "The Nobility and Gentry." As a matter of fact it was mostly nobility with a few lesser royalties thrown in. In his day he had attended to his most distinguished customers himself, and kept two coiffeured young Frenchmen to look after any he had not time for. When he died times were changing. The Great War was being fought, and his customers were bobbing their hair. (It was supposed it was the shock of this that killed him.) After the Great War, when Mr. Pert patched and remoulded what remained of the business, he found things had changed even more than he supposed. He at once grasped what was needed. No good waiting about for his father's old customers who were half of them dead or impoverished. He must attract their children and grandchildren, and even actresses if it could be managed.

The result was the present Maison Pertinax. Staffed by girls in pale grey overalls. Everywhere enamel and chromium. In every compartment an ashtray. If Mr. Pert shuddered he kept his shudders to himself; if this was what the new generations wanted, let them have it, at least he was making money. Only on royal occasions did he come into his own. Then, with a gleam in his eye he received from jewellers' messengers' heavy jewel-cases. Alone in his office he would take out of them cumbersome coronets, and stroke them with a gleam in his eye. Then later he would get into a taxi and hurry off with his curling irons in a case beside him. And for one glorious night he would coif and curl and try and pretend he was back in the days when ladies never forgot their chief glory was their hair.

Naturally the staff knew nothing of what Mr. Pert thought. To them he was "Old Pert" and a slave-driver. Sometimes Ann wondered about him. She had seen the respect with which he greeted quite shabby-looking people, while he was positively offhand with a smart young duchess.

"That was one of our old sort," she had heard him say to Miss Briggs.

"Looks a bit down at heel, poor old trout," Miss Briggs had answered.

Ann had surprised a most unchristian look in Mr. Pert's eye.

It was two minutes to nine when Ann reached the shop. Mrs. Blow, the charlady, was laying down a strip of dust-sheet.

"Now, dear," she said, "step on that. I don't want Mr. Pert to find a lot of wet footmarks when he comes."

Miss Grey was already at her desk. She nodded at Ann. "Good morning!"

Lila Grey was not popular with the staff. She was known by them as Nosey P. She was efficient, none of them denied that. But her efficiency went further than they thought necessary. It was bad enough that Mr. Pert couldn't bear to see them sit down for a minute, but when Lila Grey had to harry them as well, it was a bit too much. Then she was anything but on the staff's side. Let her overhear a bit of conversation not meant for her which might interest Mr. Pert and she could not run fast enough to his office to tell him about it.

As always happens when there is someone about with a pull, Lila Grey had plenty of people to soft-soap her. This made Ann sick. To hear what the girls said about Lila downstairs and then see the way they sucked up to her upstairs she thought revolting. For herself she had as little to do with her as she could.

"Good morning," she returned politely, and walked on.

Lila looked after her.

"I don't like that girl," she thought. Then she frowned at the engagement book. With the hairdressing girls it was easy to punish any little sign of independence. They might be sure any new customer was not for them, and down went their percentage at the end of the week. But the beauty specialists were different. There were only two of them. Such customers as Miss Briggs did not serve, Ann did. There was no argument about that, but it never stopped annoying Lila.

The girls' changing-room was in the basement. The basement was a hangover from the days of old Thomas Pert. The chromium and enamel had not crept down there. The only signs of the movement of time were a small gas stove, and lockers round the wall. Mr. Pert had fought about giving into whims of a female staff, but he had discovered that women were much easier to handle when they had somewhere to make pots of tea, and some place to keep their things which could be locked.

Ann was not the first arrival; two of the hairdressing girls were before her. Iris and Connie. Iris and Connie were friends by circumstance rather then by choice. They were the doubtful characters of the shop. The other girls got on with them all right but never felt at ease with them enough to become friends. They lived such dashing lives. They went to the same clubs and restaurants as the clients. They had incredible clothes which the simplest mathematics proved were never bought out of their salaries.

"Hullo," said Ann. "You're early."

Iris was combing her platinum curls.

"It's Connie, the old cow. I promised I'd do her hair."

Connie was changing her shoes.

"I did yours on Monday, didn't I? It's old Pert's fault. I can't see why us girls can't do each other's hair any time we're slack. This not starting after nine and not before six gets me down."

"I'd risk it"—Iris dabbed some powder on her nose—"if only Nosey P would be late for a change."

"Catch her." Connie took her overall out of her locker. "Old sour-puss."

There was a clatter on the stairs and Norah, one of the manicurists, came bounding down.

"And is it wet? I'd say the blessed saints were weeping tears over the world this morning."

Iris considered a manicurist, and a new one from some obscure place in Ireland, beneath her notice. She lifted a finger to Connie.

"Come on, you misery. If you want anything done to that henna'd tow of yours, you better step on it."

Norah stared after them with rounded eyes.

"Would that be true what she was saying?"

"What, that her hair's henna'd?" Ann buttoned her overall with some difficulty over the thickness of her frock. "Yes. But there's no harm. Mr. Pert likes us to make the best of ourselves. I bet he won't think I'm doing that this morning."

Norah, who was changing her shoes, looked up and laughed.

"In that dress you look like a pig my father would be fattening for Christmas." She stretched over to pick up her house shoes. "But don't you be troubling, allanah. What you put on your back will never be mattering, for it's charm you have shining through you."

If anybody else had said a sloppy thing like that Ann would have retorted, "Shut up!" or "Oh, yeah!" But Norah was so obviously unconscious she had said anything unusual she simply could not. As it happened she was saved answering, for at that moment the rest of the hairdressing girls, Biddy, June, Kitty and Agnes, came flying in, followed by Betty, the other manicurist.

"Heard the news?" asked Biddy.

Ann combed her hair.

"No. What?"

"Minnie Briggs has got influenza."

"She's just telephoned to Nosey P," June explained.

Kitty hung up her coat.

"And Nosey P is in a proper flap-doodle. She can't get Old Pert on the 'phone as he's already started."

Agnes took her glasses off and cleaned them with her handkerchief.

"Do you think they'll send you down to do the bride's face, Ann?"

"I bet they don't," Biddy broke in. "Lady Manton doesn't think anybody under forty knows how to do anything."

Ann's heart gave a sickening bump. Surely she wouldn't be sent down to a castle today, would she? Not a day when she'd got on these clothes! But if not her, who else? Lady Mona would have to have her face done.

"My goodness, I hope they don't! Look"—she unbuttoned her overall—"Cousin Jane's leavings. Warm, but not a wedding garment."

"Perhaps," Betty suggested, "if you go, you won't have to take off your coat."

Ann made a face at her locker.

"My mackintosh. My worst hat, and the clodhoppers mother made me buy when I had that cold."

"Girls!" Lila's voice came angrily down the stairs, "Do you know it's five-past nine and not one of you in the shop. Ann, you've been loitering nearly ten minutes."

"Coming," said Ann.

Biddy blew a kiss in the direction of Lila.

"Bless her dear little heart! How I'd like to have hold of it and give it a good pinch."

The routine at The Maison Pertinax never varied. At nine o'clock all the staff except Lila Grey set the shop to rights. If a girl was having her hair done by a friend they two had to arrange with two others to do their work on the swap system. You do mine today. I'll do yours tomorrow.

Dressing the shop was work they all hated, and vaguely resented. Naturally the dust covers had to be taken off everything. The showcases arranged. Brushes and combs set out. Bottles of shampoo filled. But they were boring jobs, and the girls felt they were doing work which was not theirs. They were glad when at ten o'clock the first customers began to arrive and they could be the starched, polished-looking Maison Pertinax girls. Shop dressing was made worse than it need have been by Lila. Of all times in the day it was the hour she liked best. Mr. Pert was not yet in the shop. She was in sole authority. Hers was an ego that fed on power. She liked to dart from cubicle to cubicle.

"Biddy and Kitty, I'm sure we're all very interested in what you did last night, but Mr. Pert pays you to work, not to gossip."

"Really, Norah, if you can't be tidier I shall report you to Mr. Pert. Drips of enamel all over this tray."

"Agnes, please come and polish this mirror. It's a disgrace."

"Iris and Connie, you might remember that some people have been decently brought up. If you must whisper things like that, you should be careful nobody can overhear you."

"Betty, come here at once. You've a button off your overall. Go down and put on another. Don't let me have to complain again."

Only Miss Briggs and Ann were free from her tongue. Miss Briggs methodically checking her stock, seeing that her own and Ann's pots of cream and lotions were full. Ann whipping off dustsheets. Straightening the couches in the two cubicles. Polishing the mirrors. Laying out swabs. Filling the thermos containers with ice. Sorting and tidying both their make-up tables. Miss Briggs had never given Ann an order after her first week in the shop. She believed in leaving competent people alone to do their own work.

Lila with no such inhibitions seized on Miss Briggs's absence to harry Ann. She came and stood in the door of her cubicle.

"Put that cover straight." She pointed to the perfectly smoothly folded rug. "Miss Briggs, as I expect you've heard, has influenza, but that's no reason for you to scamp your work."

Ann paused in what she was doing and looked at Lila in assumed surprise.

"Of course not. Did you think it was?"

In the other cubicles the girls paused to listen. Biddy's head poked round Kitty's curtain.

"Hark at old Ann. I bet she tells Nosey P where she gets off."

"Don't be impertinent, Ann," said Lila.

Ann smiled sweetly.

"Of course not."

"What's that doing here?" Lila pointed to a bottle of milk on the table. "You know you mustn't bring food into the shop."

Ann blinked at the milk.

"Food? But I don't eat make-up."

There was a sound of giggling from the other cubicles. Lila flushed. How stupid of her to have forgotten that some facials needed milk.

"If that milk is for your work, you should put it in a proper container."

"Of course," Ann agreed.

Lila could have hit her. Instead she resolved to punish her another way. She would not hand on Miss Briggs's message to Mr. Pert. She would keep back that part which said Ann was perfectly competent to take her place. She would only pass on the final message. "If Ann cannot be spared, ask the Wolstone School of Beauty Culture to send one of their staff."

Somehow, in spite of Lila, a lot of news managed to be exchanged at shop-dressing time. This morning there was a growing amount of chatter. As each girl began to thaw in the warm, centrally heated air, her tongue loosed.

"I saw him again last night," Biddy told Kitty. "He said what about our doing a bit of Lambeth Walking on Saturday?"

"Thought you were going out with Bert," Kitty objected.

"Oh, him!" Biddy dismissed Bert with a shrug. "He's a good old stodge. But not when there's anything better about. No, sir!"

Kitty sighed, and said nothing. Biddy's ability to have all the young men in her neighbourhood waiting in queues for her, filled her with hopeless admiration. She had only her Tom. Nobody could be nicer than Tom, but he hadn't much money, and he wasn't always free at the weekends. He had a mother who kept him in.

"She makes me so nervous," Betty whispered to Norah. "I just drop things when she comes round."

"Her!" Norah looked in supreme disdain in the direction of Lila. "I'd not be caring what was thought by the likes of her."

"I said to him," said Iris, putting the drier over Connie's well-set head, "Well, I do catch cold easily. The doctor says I ought to have a fur coat. But where can a girl like me get a fur coat?"

Connie held one ear out of the drier.

"Did he bite?"

Iris gave her a nudge.

"Might even be mink."

Agnes and June met over the shampoo containers.

"Do you think I've taken off a bit?" June asked, turning sideways. "I was at The League last night and I can hold my toes now and put my forehead on my knees. They say that's wonderful for the waistline."

Agnes peered at her through her glasses.

"You still stick out a bit. Perhaps it's your belt, though."

"Belt!" June patted her front. "I don't wear a belt. What I says is, it's hard enough on your feet standing about here. But if it's going to be hard on my stomach, too, squeezing it into a belt, then I give up."

Ann, alone in her cubicle with no friendly outspoken Minnie Briggs to say a word to, was full of thoughts. She must manage to send Min a few flowers. Wasn't much fun having influenza alone in your flat. She would go and see her if it wasn't that she might catch it and give it to Bunny. Pity it was Wednesday. She had only just enough money to see her through to the end of the week. But somehow she must squeeze out a one and sixpence. Get a nice lot of anemones for that. She would go out in her dinner hour and buy them, and tell the shop to send them. She'd think how she was going to manage without the one and sixpence later.

As the clock struck a quarter to ten, Mr. Pert opened the shop door. Even in the street Mr. Pert looked a hairdresser. It took no imagination to picture a comb sticking out of his breast pocket. From his neat little moustache down to his neat, rather pointed shoes he looked one who at any moment might click his tongue against his teeth, and say, "The scalp isn't at all as I like to see it. Not at all."

Lila Grey rose from her desk as he came in. She came towards him exuding bad news before she opened her mouth. Mr. Pert was shaking his umbrella on the mat. He looked up.

"Is something wrong?"

Lila's voice had a decidedly cemetery tone.

"Miss Briggs has influenza."

"Dear, dear!" Mr. Pert bustled across the shop to a small glass partitioned corner he used as an office. "Come in, Miss Grey. Now, what about the Manton wedding?"

"Miss Briggs had thought of that. She suggests we telephone the Wolstone School of Beauty Culture. She says for so exceptional an occasion they would send one of their staff."

Mr. Pert moved his shoulders angrily. If he had been a cat his fur would have stood on end.

"Ridiculous! I've no intention of sending anyone but one of my own girls. It's inconvenient as it leaves us with nobody here, but that girl, Ann Lane, must go."

"But—" Lila broke in.

"I know," Mr. Pert agreed. "It's unfortunate about our clients here, but the Manton family have been served by our family for two generations—"

"But," Lila interrupted again, "is Ann suitable? I mean, a wedding's an important day. Lady Mona will want her face just right."

Mr. Pert looked surprised.

"But Ann Lane is very good at her work. Miss Briggs has told me so frequently. Please send her in to me."

Lila, bottling up her fury, went to Ann's cubicle.

Ann looked up as Lila came in.

"Don't tell me. I've got to do Lady Mona."

Lila stiffened.

"You take a good deal for granted. As a matter of fact, yes. I've persuaded Mr. Pert to give you this chance. Go and see him at once."

Ann gave a quick look at herself in the glass to see she was tidy. She straightened her overall. She was not going to give Lila the pleasure of knowing she did not want to go.

"Right," she said, and went out.

CHAPTER TWO

ANN rubbed the steaming pane of the carriage window with her mackintosh sleeve. Through the sleet-clogged glass she could see the curving lines of the South Downs. Goodness, she must be nearly at Lewes. Her heart beat a little faster. She was not naturally more shy than most people. But in her ugliest and clumsiest clothes she did wish the being met by the chauffeur and the getting into the castle were over, and she safely in her overall at work on Lady Mona's face. "Of course," as she kept saying to herself, "it was perfectly ridiculous to be scared of people like chauffeurs and butlers—after all, they were just men like dad or anybody else. All the same," the least brave part of her retorted, "if I've got to talk to them I do wish I looked nicer. I hate people peering down their noses at me."

At Lewes station there seemed to be a lot of people meeting everybody, but no chauffeur. Then suddenly she was touched on the elbow. A kind-faced elderly man in chauffeur's uniform was beside her.

"Are you the young lady for The Castle?"

"Yes," Ann agreed, "from Maison Pertinax."

He looked down at her little case which held her makeup and overall.

"Give me that."

Ann laughed.

"Doesn't weigh anything. You'd look silly carrying it. Where's the car?"

He pointed up the stairs.

"Outside. This way."

Ann felt she was being made a fool of. She was settled into the corner of a Rolls Royce. The chauffeur with care tucked an immense fur rug round her knees. Since she had been quite small she had been an independent person doing things for herself. Never, except when she was ill, had she been tucked and patted like this. "Must have an idea I'm made of butter," she thought, feeling rather embarrassed. She marvelled at the rich who could put up with being messed about like this every time they went out.

The Castle was a show place. It had been built at the time of the Norman Conquest. Some of the walls were left and the moat. Even seeing it on a day of blinding sleet, Ann caught her breath at its loveliness. She longed to call out to the chauffeur "Stop a minute and let me look."

The car drew up at the great front door which looked like the entrance to a church. Ann threw the rug off her knees, picked up her case, and scrambled out. The chauffeur was ringing the bell. He looked at her in surprise.

"You should wait in the car. The butler may take a minute answering. You'll get wet."

Ann laughed.

"I've already walked part of the way to work this morning. A little more won't hurt me."

The chauffeur's kind eyes rested on her.

"A few of those I drive about ought to hear you. Do them good."

The door opened. All Ann's feeling of inferiority returned at sight of the butler. He was just the sort of butler you see in an American-made film. A figure of immense dignity whose face even in repose looked as you would expect the Archbishop of Canterbury's to look at a royal church event.

"Here's the young lady, Mr. Hall," the chauffeur said.

The butler looked at Ann as if he had never before seen any one so unworthy of notice.

"The young person from The Maison Pertinax?"

Ann longed to say "I can look nicer than this. I've only got them on because it's wet and cold."

Instead she agreed humbly that she was the young person.

"Lady Mona is waiting." The butler turned. "Follow me."

As Ann went in she looked over her shoulder to smile "goodbye" to the chauffeur. She supposed she must have made a mistake but she could almost swear he winked.

Lady Mona was in bed. She was sitting propped up with innumerable cushions. Wearing a little quilted coat over emerald green satin pyjamas. Her mother, the Marchioness, was sitting on the end of the bed. Ann in one startled glance saw that the room was of a gorgeousness she had never before visualised.

"Hullo," said Mona. "I'm sorry Miss Briggs is ill but I'd rather it was you. I only asked for her because she usually does me and I thought she might be hurt."

The Marchioness got up.

"Now I want you to be very careful, Miss Lane. I know what you young girls are. Too much of everything. Remember this is a country wedding. Make-up that shows would be most out of place."

"Don't fuss, Mother," Mona objected. "What d'you think I want to look like? Jezebel?"

"No, dear, of course not. But with Miss Briggs I knew I could trust her to use her discretion. Most unfortunate."

"Shut up, duckie." Mona turned to Ann. "I've had that table there cleared for you. Will that be all right?"

Ann looked at the table and saw it was just what she needed.

"Yes, my Lady. Shall I start now?"

"Hop it, Mother." Mona jerked her head towards the door. "When I'm massaged I like to be alone."

"Quite right, my darling. You rest." The Marchioness gave her daughter a kiss. She nodded at Ann. "Please don't talk to her, Miss Lane. I want her to relax. Her lunch is coming up at one o'clock which will give us nice time in which to dress her."

Mona watched Ann set out her creams and lotions, take off her outdoor things and put on her overall.

"Did you mind coming?" she asked suddenly.

Ann caught unawares spoke the truth.

"I wished it hadn't been today. Or that I'd known. I've got all my awfulest clothes on."

"What's it matter?"

Ann laid out some squares of cotton wool and wheeled the table to the side of the bed.

"When there's butlers and people you can't help wishing you didn't look a worm."

Mona giggled.

"Hall? Don't fuss about him. He's an old fool."

Ann examined the bed with an experienced eye.

"Do you mind lying at the wrong end. I can't get at you with that canopy thing."

"Course not." Mona got out of bed. "Just put me where you want me."

Ann rearranged the bed. Then she settled Mona. She took a lump of cream in her fingers and began her work.

"What a louse of a day," said Mona. "I wish it was sunny. I feel depressed in this."

Ann massaged soothingly.

"What's it matter as long as you're marrying the person you want to?"

There was silence for a moment, then to Ann's surprise two tears rolled out from underneath Mona's eyelids.

"Goodness," said Ann, all her professional instincts aroused. "Don't cry, you'll make an awful mess of your face."

Mona giggled through her tears.

"It's you saying that. I am so fond of Tony. But these last days it's just been fuss, fuss, fuss. I've hardly seen him. And I'm so tired I feel I'll be a bore on my honeymoon. I hardly slept at all last night."

Ann's fingers felt for and found the little nest of nerves on either side of the forehead. Gently she massaged them. Even while she worked she could feel Mona relax.

"I always think," Ann said, "that though a big wedding looks awfully nice, a little one and no fuss would be the sort I should like."

Mona, soothed, murmured:

"That's nice. Go on." Then after a pause. "Go on talking. Tell me about you. When did you learn to do this?"

Ann took some more cream.

"At a place called The Wolstone School of Beauty Culture. I was there six months."

"Did you have to pay to learn?"

Ann smiled.

"Of course. It was expensive. Fifty pounds." She saw Mona smile. "Well, that's expensive to us. Besides it didn't stop there. You have to get everything yourself. Overalls. Towels. Face Bandages. Grease. Make-up. Manicure things. Eyebrow tweezers. There's no end to it. We reckoned the extras cost another fifteen pounds."

"What did you do?"

Ann's fingers moved with an increasingly soothing motion.

"Everything. Have to learn all about the face. Skin. Bone structure. Nerves and muscles. You have to write a paper on it. Then of course there's all the different sorts of treatment besides ordinary massage."

"Do you get paid a lot? You ought to."

Ann went back to her gentle manipulation of the little over-tight nerve groups on either side of the forehead.

"I will. Now I'm only beginning so I get thirty-five shillings a week. When I've been at it longer I'll get as much as three pounds ten."

"Thirty-five shillings! What on earth can you do with that?"

Ann laughed.

"Quite a lot. But there's more than that. We get a percentage of one and eight in the pound on all our work and what we sell."

"And tips." Mona's voice was drowsy.

"And tips," Ann agreed. She leaned over and looked at Mona's eyelids. The eyelashes were still. She dropped her voice to a whisper. "Quite a lot sometimes. Half-a-crown. Once I got five shillings—"

She stopped talking but her fingers went on working. Each nerve and muscle she picked out and kneaded. There would be no signs of tiredness this afternoon.

Ann massaged for half an hour. She kept glancing at the clock. "I shall have to wake her at half-past twelve," she thought. "I must give her a bit of an astringent to get rid of all this cream and there's her make-up." She looked regretfully at the eyebrow pluckers she had meant to use. "Oh, well," she told herself resignedly, "this sleep's worth more than the full massage she's missed. And a few eyebrows too many won't show."

Just before half-past twelve Mona opened her eyes. She blinked at Ann.

"Have I been asleep?"

Ann nodded.

"Half an hour. Feel better?"

Mona stretched like a cat.

"Divine. I feel so placid I don't think I'd fuss if I fell into a puddle in my wedding dress."

Ann plastered milk on her face.

"Ouch," Mona shuddered. "That's cold."

Ann stood back for the milk to dry.

"What are your bridesmaids wearing?"

"It's a harlequin affair. They are all anemone shades, in velvet. Two lavender. Two dark blue. Two purple. Two fuchsia. They are carrying flat baskets of anemones and wreaths of anemones on their heads."

"Sounds lovely."

Mona nodded.

"They are and so's mine. I'll show you that. It's marvellous they are so good, for a perfectly frightful cousin of mine called Dennis runs a dress shop, and he designed them."

Ann took up a pad of cotton wool to take off the milk. Then she paused with it in the air staring at the door. There was a tremendous commotion in the passage—a high male voice shouted:

"But she's got to know sometime, Aunt. I shall tell her myself. I'll have hysterics if something isn't done soon."

"Be quiet." Came the Marchioness' voice hushed but furious. "She's relaxing while her face is done. I don't want her disturbed."

"Then I shall have hysterics."

Mona looked at Ann.

"That's Dennis. I bet the anemones haven't arrived or something." She sat up in bed. "Dennis," she called. "Come in. I can hear you very well out there but you may as well save your voice."

Immediately the door burst open and Dennis followed by the Marchioness followed by Mona's maid almost fell in.

"It's too, too frightful," said Dennis.

"Save up the sob stuff and let's hear," Mona suggested.

"There's not the least need to bother, dear Mona," the Marchioness objected. "It can be settled quite easily without her."

"Quite easily!" Dennis raised two anguished arms to the ceiling. "I suppose you simply don't care that my months and months of work are wasted. Simply wasted."

Mona lay down again. She looked up at Ann.

"May as well get my face done. I don't gather anything's happened to Tony and that's all I care about."

Dennis came over and shook her arm.

"Don't you care if your wedding's ruined?"

Mona grinned at him.

"Perhaps I will, duckie, when I know what the trouble is. But I don't suppose so. She—" She pointed at Ann, "massaged me so beautifully I went to sleep and now I don't care about anything."

The Marchioness sat on the bed.

"That's a very good thing, dear, because it is really most unfortunate news. I didn't mean to tell you. But Dennis won't have his wedding procession upset. Sally is ill. She can't be a bridesmaid this afternoon."

"Sally!" Mona sat up. "Poor sweet. She was all right when she arrived last night."

The Marchioness nodded.

"She was taken ill in the night. Violent sickness. She thought it was something she had eaten. Early this morning she became worse and rang for Manners." She glanced at the maid who stepped forward.

"Oh, she was bad, my lady. I got Mr. Hall up and he telephoned for the doctor."

Mona looked at her mother. "What did he say?"

"He wasn't sure at first, but about an hour ago they took her away in an ambulance. It's appendicitis. They're operating now."

"Poor old Sally," Mona said. "Still, if she doesn't have a worse time with hers than I had with mine she won't be so bad. Well finish the old face, Miss Lane." She looked at Dennis. "Don't get in an uproar. I'll be married just the same even if the procession is a bit lop-sided."

The Marchioness was relieved.

"That's splendid of you, dear. I knew you'd be sensible."

"Sensible," Dennis shrieked. "What about me? This wedding was my piece de resistance."

"Oh, stow it, Dennis," said Mona. "Piece de resistance my foot."

"You don't understand, any of you." Dennis was almost in tears. "This was a work of art. A crescendo in anemones. You must put someone else in Sally's place. I can't have my work ruined."

Mona made a despairing shrug to her mother.

"Hark at him. You'd think bridesmaids grew in the hedges in Sussex." She turned back to Dennis. "You forget where we are. Even if we went as far as Lewes I don't know anyone who'd do."

Dennis' face was white with anxiety.

"But you must. Think. Hasn't someone got a daughter?"

"Dozens have." Mona closed her eyes for Ann to make up her lids. "But all the wrong shape. I can't think of one we know who'd fit. Sally's small and slight. She's about the size of Miss Lane."

The Marchioness looked at Ann.

"Thinner. Much."

Ann realised her figure had nothing to do with the discussion. But she did not care for the Marchioness's tone.

"I'm not as fat as I look. It's my frock, my lady."

Dennis caught his breath.

"Take it off."

Ann saw he was looking at her.

"Take what off?"

"Your frock, your overall. Everything."

"Really, Dennis." The Marchioness was shocked. "I know you are upset but that's no way to talk to Miss Lane, even in fun."

"Fun," Dennis gasped. "It's not fun. Don't you see that if she's thin enough she'll do."

The Marchioness snorted.

"Really, Dennis!"

Mona sat up. She turned round and gripped hold of Ann.

"Don't snort, Mother. Dennis is quite right. She will do." She sprang out of bed. "Clear out, Mother, and take Dennis with you. Manners, go and fetch Miss Sally's frock. Quick."

Almost before they knew it Mona had pushed her mother and Dennis into the passage, and had sent Manners flying. Then with dancing eyes she turned to Ann.

"What fun. I'd adore to have you as a bridesmaid. Take off your things."

"But—" Ann began.

"Don't argue. Strip."

Ann, almost stunned by the sudden turn of events, obediently took off her overall. Then her frock. Then suddenly she turned crimson. The long glass beside her showed her not in the pretty camiknickers made by herself that she usually wore, but in the old woollen knickers (a leftover from her school days), that she had put on that day for extra warmth. Even her legs which were really lovely looked at their worst in the clodhopping shoes.

Mona saw the flush and understood. She dashed to a cupboard and pulled out a shelf. From it she selected white satin knickers and a satin slip. She threw them to Ann.

"Put them on."

At that moment the door opened and Manners came in. Over her arm lay a frock. In her hand were two boxes.

Almost everybody has a frock of which they dream. Ann had always loved blue. She had planned that some day she would buy a blue evening dress. An evening dress that she could afford would be a cheap affair in taffeta perhaps. But cheap or not she had always known just how it would look. It would be a darkish blue, with bouffant skirts and lovely gleams of colour in the folds.

The dress Manners carried was blue. It was the colour of a dark blue anemone. It had immensely full skirts. It was made of chiffon velvet so soft it seemed as if you could pass it through a ring. It was Ann's dream dress glorified, but come true.

Manners was a personal maid because she loved her work. She had been glad to come to Mona because as she said "she paid to dress." One glance at Ann showed her that Ann "paid to dress" too. In a moment she had laid the bridesmaid's frock over a chair, and was undressing her.

"Let me, Miss."

Ann was terribly embarrassed. No one except her mother had ever seen her with no clothes on. No one, not even her mother had undressed her since she had got past being laid across somebody's knee. But to Manners and Mona bodies meant nothing. Manners stripped everything off her, and Mona watched. Manners and Mona discussed her redressing as if she were not there.

"What about a little silk vest, my lady. She's so slim it'll never show. And it'll be cold getting in and out of a car."

"Yes. One of those very thin ones," Mona agreed.

On went the vest. On went a tiny satin girdle.

"Of course the stockings won't show," said Manners. "But I'd say those pale flesh you got in Paris, my lady."

Mona nodded.

"Yes. I hope the shoes fit. She's got tiny feet."

On went the stockings. Manners would not even let Ann fasten the suspenders.

"You let me."

On went the satin knickers. On went the slip. Then Manners took the lid off one of the two boxes. She took out velvet shoes to match the frock.

It was like the shoe-fitting scene in Cinderella. Mona and Manners knelt on the floor at Ann's feet.

"Too big," said Manners. "Not much though. I could make them all right with a bit of cotton wool in the toe, my lady."

Mona pressed her finger on the space where Ann's toes should have been.

"I think you better give her some ribbon as well. It'll never show under the frock."

The shoe problem settled, Manners breathing through the nose with excitement took the frock off the bed and put it over Ann's head.

There can be no nicer moment in a person's life than when they put on a really perfect frock. Ann could see herself in the long glass. She could see the soft curves of lovely blue. Could see the tight fitting bodice. The long sleeves. The high neck. The enormous skirts with gleams of brighter blue in the folds. Manners was behind doing up the buttons so she could not see how enchanting Ann looked but Mona could.

"Oh," was all she said. Then again. "Oh!"

Manners never had cared to see her work until she could as she said "see it of a piece." Keeping her eyes from Ann she opened the other box. From it came the anemone wreath. She handed it to Ann.

"You put this on, Miss. Use her ladyship's comb."

The wreath was easy to wear. Ann's brown curls fitted into the flowers. Her centre parting suited the line of the wreath. The sight of the flowers though brought her back to reality. Could this be her? The Ann who this very morning had stopped at a florist on her way to the station and sent anemones to Minnie Briggs? She turned to Mona and Manners with a quick movement that flared out her skirt.

"I can't do this. It's ridiculous." She looked pleadingly at Mona. "You must see how unsuitable it is?"

As far as Mona and Manners were concerned Ann might not have spoken. To them she was the doll they had dressed. They were overcome by their handiwork.

"Oh, my lady," Manners gasped. "Doesn't she look sweet. There's none of the other young ladies will look better."

Mona beamed at Ann.

"You look a pet. Go on, Manners, fetch in her ladyship and Mr. Dennis."

Dennis, forgetting all manners, pushed past his Aunt and pranced into the room. Inside he stood suddenly still.

"Primavera."

"That's it." Mona turned in triumph to Manners. "She was the goddess of spring."

"Does look spring-like doesn't she, sir." Manners agreed. "It's the flowers I think. I always say nothing like a few flowers about you to make you feel winter's over."

Ann looked past the three rapturous faces to the Marchioness and there saw her salvation. She went over to her.

"Please, my lady, make them see it won't do. I can't be a bridesmaid. I don't belong here."

The Marchioness's face softened.

"You look perfectly charming, my dear child. But you're right. It can't be."

Mona came over to her mother.

"But why not? I'm sure Miss Lane is just the sort of person I'd choose for a bridesmaid."

The Marchioness sat on the bed. Her voice was quiet and reasonable.

"Look here, my dear. You are only having eight girls. Because Dennis was so anxious for the beauty of the ceremony you had to leave out a lot of people that you should have asked. It's not our fault that poor Sally is ill, but when the guests learn you've got a complete stranger as a bridesmaid it's bound to give offence."

"You're thinking of Aunt Lisa and those awful girls."

"Well, they are your first cousins. If only you would have had one of them."

"They're such a terrible shape."

"I know," the Marchioness agreed. "All the same they are hurt. It was bad enough you were having Sally, a girl none of them knew."

"Well, she was at school with me."

"Yes, but a South African. I think she's charming but she was not of your circle. Now if you have Miss Lane you'll make things worse. Your Aunt Lisa doesn't seem to realise what shape her girls are. She's sure to think one of them could have worn the frock. When I have to explain that you used Miss Lane from the hairdressers you know what a scene there'll be."

"But why should we say who Miss Lane is? That's our business. You say nobody knew Sally. Well, let them think Miss Lane is her."

The Marchioness's face changed.

"Well, that would be a way out of the difficulty." She turned to Ann. "What is your name, dear?"

"Ann."

"Would you mind being Sally for this one afternoon? The real Sally's surname is Groot but you needn't use that. Everyone will think you are Sally. They'll probably call you Sally for they've all heard you were coming over for the wedding. You needn't actually tell a he about it. But just accept the name."

Ann looked round the faces. Manners, Dennis, Mona, the Marchioness. They all eyed her expectantly.

"Very well, my lady."

"Kind child. Now you must drop this 'my lady' right away. You must call me Lady Manton and Mona by her Christian name." She turned to Manners. "Take the child's dress off and see she has lunch."

"With me," Mona interrupted.

"I must go and find Hall. He must see that all the servants understand they are to say nothing about what's happened. Come along, Dennis."

Manners removed Ann's wedding garments. She put her into a silk dressing-gown. Left alone the two girls stared at each other. Then suddenly Mona threw her arms round Ann and kissed her.

"Isn't this fun, Sally-Ann?"

CHAPTER THREE

Lead us, heavenly Father, lead us
O'er the world's tempestuous sea.

With her eyes cast down Ann walked up the aisle. She felt desperately shy. The orbs of the relations and friends in the congregation seemed to pierce her neck. She could imagine them nudging each other and whispering "She's a friend." The drive to the church had been a nightmare. Manners had told her who her fellow bridesmaids would be. Lady Jane and Lady Primrose Fain in lavender and the Honourable Cora Bolt in blue like herself, had been the ones who drove with her. The Marchioness had been very neat in her introduction. The other seven girls had been in the hall when she came down. She had put her hand on her shoulder.

"This is Sally, my dears. And now you must be off."

In the car the other three had fired a few remarks at her.

"You're from South Africa aren't you?"

Ann nodded.

"You and Mona were at school together in Paris?"

Ann nodded again, nods she felt were less lies than words.

"What was it like? Mona said you had an awfully good time."

Ann took a deep breath. It was the first she had heard of a school in Paris. She did hope they weren't going to start talking French.

"It was fun."

She felt her monosyllabic answers and nods were surprising the others. She did not look up but she sensed they were raising their eyebrows. She felt sorry for the absent Sally who was getting a reputation for dumbness, but not for her or anybody else was she going to get led into a discussion of schools and places she had never seen.

The other girls talked amongst themselves. The great excitement seemed to be the state of the roads, there was a bridesmaids' dance in town that night. Would they or wouldn't they be fit to drive on after the wedding.

Ann left to herself took the chance to examine the others. Lady Primrose was the one beside her and Lady Jane was on the seat in front of her. All she knew about them was that their father was a Duke and Manners said they were "very pleasant young ladies." Manners had been less complimentary about Cora.

"Then there's the Honourable Cora Bolt," she said. "She's Lady Mona's cousin. Very showy with red hair and great brown eyes. Always in the picture papers. You must have seen her. Lady Mona had her for a bridesmaid for she'll look so well, but she can't abide her really. Sly as you make them. Like that as a child they say. The housekeeper here tells me she's known her since she was a baby and she'd never trust her farther than she could throw her."

Ann looked at Cora. Cora was on the seat in front of Primrose. Ann got a very good view of her profile. She certainly was lovely. Curls of real red gold. The pink and white complexion only the luckiest of redheads is blessed with. Huge brown eyes surrounded with long curling lashes.

As if she sensed that Ann was studying her she looked at her over her shoulder.

"You're walking with me. You're on the left."

"She's not, Cora," Primrose objected. "She's behind me." She turned to Ann.

"We had a rehearsal yesterday before you arrived." Jane laughed.

"Dennis nearly had hysterics when he heard you wouldn't arrive until too late. He said we were to see you stood behind Primrose."

Primrose nodded.

"Just an arms-length. You never heard such a fuss. I've been a bridesmaid eight times. I don't need telling. Do you?"

Cora turned pink.

"You're wrong though. I was behind you."

Primrose shrugged her shoulders and grinned at her sister.

"You'll see him just as well, dear, from the left. And he can't see you any way. Best men always have their backs to the bridesmaids."

"Idiots." Cora managed to sound casual. "What the hell do I care about Timothy? But I was behind Primrose."

"Give in to her," Jane said to Ann. "Once Cora makes up her mind it's less trouble to oblige."

Ann did not care where she walked. In spite of the wet an enormous crowd had assembled outside the church and all down the village street to watch the bride and her maids arrive. All the picture papers had sent cameramen. The other three girls seemed used to being stared at, openly discussed, and photographed. But Ann was not. When at last she had walked up the red carpet under the awning, she was crimson-faced, and her heart was beating like a tom-tom. To be left alone in a dark corner of the porch to recover was all she wanted. Nothing mattered to her less then whether she walked on Cora's left or right.

With a good deal of nudging and whispering the girls got into line, five each side of the porch, and waited for Mona. Jane, who was in front of Ann, turned to her.

"I wish I wasn't me. I'm principal bridesmaid. I've got to jump forward at the right moment and grab Mona's lilies. I always was a fool at that sort of thing but balancing a bouquet of lilies as well as this damn basket of anemones is a bit thick." Then she nudged Ann. "Here's Dennis. Stand straight and look pretty."

Dennis glanced up and down the lines, cooing.

"Exquisite! Too divine, darling." Then suddenly his eye lit on Sally.

"You're wrong. Did I put you there?"

Jane answered for her.

"She wasn't at the rehearsal."

"Darling!" He took Ann's arm. "Over here. Cora goes behind Jane. My conception is a poem of blended hair tones."

Cora changed places with Ann. Most unjustly Ann thought she gave her a nasty look. After all it wasn't her who was planning the procession.

"Looks sour, doesn't she," Primrose whispered. "As a matter of fact I hear—"

But what Primrose had heard Ann never knew. For at that moment the choir and clergy came down to the porch. Two minutes later shouts of "good luck" in the village street and a buzz of talk outside showed that Mona had arrived.

"—that you may so live together in this life, that in the world to come ye may have life everlasting."

The Bishop (Uncle of the bridegroom), who was saying part of the marriage service turned and led the way to the altar. Mona and Tony stepped forward to follow him. It was then Ann saw that there was going to be a tragedy. Jane had not stepped back far enough when she collected Mona's lilies. Her foot was on the train and still worse on the veil.

Quick as lightning Ann caught Jane by the arm. She pulled her back. Simultaneously, Timothy, the best man, had spotted what was about to happen. He wasted no time but gave Jane a good shove from the front. Jane whose mind had been miles away and who had been gazing abstract-edly at the East window was taken completely unawares. She tottered and would have fallen if Timothy, having got her safely off the train, had not gripped her arm and Ann supported her from behind. It was all done so quickly that no one except the other bridesmaids saw what had happened.

Timothy, his immediate duties done, slipped into a pew.

It was the one next to Ann. The choir were singing a psalm. With a suitably solemn face he took up his hymn sheet. Then he looked down at Ann. At once they both remembered the swaying Jane. His face wrinkled, Ann's mouth twitched. With superhuman effort they choked down their giggles. Not once for the remainder of the service did they dare look at each other.

They met in the vestry over the signing of the register.

"Hullo, Timothy," said Cora.

Timothy in the middle of the confusion and bride kissing that was going on didn't hear her. He looked at Ann.

"Hullo, fellow-rescuer. The best man can kiss the bridesmaids. May I?"

He said it so lightly and amusingly that Ann unselfconsciously offered her cheek.

He was tall and to get down to her in that small room full of jostling people he took her by the shoulders.

"I didn't know you two knew each other." Cora's voice had an edge to it.

Timothy finished his kiss, then still holding Ann he looked over her shoulder laughing.

"We don't, my pet." Then to Ann "Who are you?"

"Sally." Even as Ann said the name she wished she might tell the truth. He looked so nice. Just the person to share the joke with. A man who laughed like that would be sure to see how funny it was that she, Ann Lane, beauty specialist of The Maison Pertinax, was being a bridesmaid at one of the smartest weddings of the year.

"Sally what?" His voice was not thin like so many voices but had warmth behind it. It made his question intimate.

"Just Sally."

His eyes looked amused.

"Just Sally?" He nodded as if he liked what he saw. "Very well 'Just Sally.' We'll meet presently."

Somebody called him to sign the register. He turned away. Ann looked after him. She felt better. Much less of a fraud. Here was someone not talking to her as a friend of Mona's, but just as Sally, somebody with whom he'd laughed over a bridesmaid's muddle.

"Vous ne jouez pas la sainte nitouche," said Cora.

Ann stared at her. She had done a little French at school, but she had never been good at it. Anyway it hadn't been that sort of French. Much more verbs and "Where is the pen of my aunt."

"Vous ne jouez la sainte nitouche," Cora repeated.

Ann looked at her rather as a bird is supposed to look at a snake. It was almost certain the absent Sally spoke French like a native. Girls who finished in Paris usually did.

"Yes, it was a pretty wedding, wasn't it," she said, hoping for the best.

Cora opened her eyes.

"What are you playing at? You heard what I said."

Ann nodded.

"I didn't understand. I've forgotten my French."

Cora opened her eyes.

"There's something queer about you. You aren't a bit how Mona always described you. And you can't have forgotten your French unless you've lost your memory. People don't who are educated entirely in France."

"All the same I have forgotten."

"I was just admiring you for not pretending to be a prude."

This was obviously a lie and Ann would have liked to have said "Oh yeah!" Instead she took advantage of the crush and moved away. But she could feel Cora's eyes on her, that

Cora's nose was sniffing at a mystery. Anyway "what a cat" she thought. After all it was the custom for the best man to kiss the bridesmaids.

Back at the castle the bridesmaids had to surround the bride and groom while they received. It was three quarters of an hour before they were free to move. At once Ann felt lonely. The other seven girls seemed to know everybody present. She knew nobody. She was tired and wished she could sit but every chair seemed to be taken. Food and drink in vast quantities was being carried round but somehow none of it got to her. Then suddenly her elbow was gripped.

"Hullo, 'Just Sally.' I've been looking for you everywhere. Mona's put you in my charge. 'What,' I said, 'giving me "Just Sally" to look after? Well I take that kindly, nothing could suit me better.'"

Ann laughed, and suddenly felt gay and like a person at a wedding.

"Didn't she look nice."

Timothy looked round the room and saw a solid gate-legged table in the corner. He steered Ann to it.

"Let's sit on this. Yes, Mona looked a peach. What about a bite and some champagne?"

Ann was doubtful.

"I've never drunk champagne. Do you think it would go to my head?"

He laughed.

"Very nicely acted, but you can't get away with that, my girl. We all know you nearly broke up Madame Moulin's school in Paris."

Ann stared down at her frock. "Gosh," she thought, "The things I'm learning about Sally."

"Oh well," she explained. "I've reformed since then."

Hall was hurrying by with a tray of glasses. Timothy caught him by the shoulder.

"Would you pass a man dying of thirst, Hall?" Hall turned at the sound of the voice, his face slightly unfrozen for a friend of the house, then he saw who else he was expected to serve. He looked even more disdainful then when he had let Ann in that morning.

"I'm sorry, Sir Timothy, I didn't see you." His tray was held well away from Ann.

Timothy took two glasses. He handed her one.

"And what shall we bite?"

Ann, absolutely tongue-tied by the presence of Hall, muttered.

"Oh, anything."

"Anything rubbish." Timothy held Hall's sleeve. "Now, Hall, fight your way to the buffet and get us at least a dozen caviar sandwiches. Miss Sally's hungry."

"Oh—" Ann protested.

Hall gave her a snubbing glance as if to say "Keep your mouth shut."

"Very good, Sir Timothy," he agreed. There was a faint inflexion of the Sir Timothy which entirely excluded Ann.

Timothy took a gulp of champagne.

"Funny old trout, Hall. Got the most disobligin' manner of any butler I know. I daresay he's all right really; good to his mother and all that, but I don't like his mug and never have."

Ann sipped her champagne. It tasted all right, but she was afraid of it. How much could you drink of it safely? How awful if she got drunk.

Timothy looked at her in amusement.

"It won't bite." Then he put his head on one side and studied her. "I believe old Mona's got you wrong. I've always heard such a lot about this tough little South African. You know, the girl from the land where the flowers have no scent, the birds no song, and the women no morals. But you don't look a bit like that."

Ann returned his look firmly.

"Why do you know people by what other people say about them? You don't look like a person who'd do that."

Timothy laid a hand over hers for a second.

"Quite right, 'Just Sally.' I deserved that. Tell me about South Africa. I've always wanted to go there."

Ann swallowed. What on earth did she know about South Africa.

"Well, there are snakes there."

He laughed.

"Listen to you. All right, if you don't want to talk about South Africa what shall we talk about?"

Ann was spared an immediate answer by the arrival of Hall. He carried the plate of sandwiches. He put them down by Timothy.

"Your sandwiches, sir."

Timothy raised his eyebrows.

"Miss Sally's sandwiches. Pass them to her."

Hall, as if he were being asked to pick up a red-hot plate, lifted it and presented it to Ann.

Ann felt she was going to laugh. Hall's face was such a study. After all why should it matter to him if she were a bridesmaid or not?

"Thank you, Hall." She took a sandwich and in taking it looked up at him for the fraction of a second. It was a "so what?" sort of glance. A little tit for tat for his snubbing manner of the morning.

Hall put the plate between them. As he moved away even his back seemed to say "Things are come to a pretty pass."

"Well," said Timothy. "You haven't answered my question."

Ann raised her eyes to his. It was an easy face to look at. He was fair, rather long about the jaw, he had very blue eyes.

"Sir" Hall had called him. He couldn't be a knight. People as young as he was didn't get knighted. He must be a baronet.

"Tell me about you. What d'you do?"

He took another sandwich.

"Don't you know?"

She shook her head.

"Why should I?"

"Only you can hardly miss it. I'm a 'Munster.' You know 'Munster the dirt away.' 'Do you feel Mondayish? Then wash our way and you'll feel Munsterish.'"

Ann leant against the wall. She had forgotten she had ever felt lonely and out of place at this wedding. She was enjoying herself.

"I know the pictures. Women all over tired lines doing the washing."

"Ah!" Timothy held up a mock protesting finger. "That's only part one. Part two shows them listening to the wireless, every care smoothed away while Munster does their work."

"As a matter of fact it is good, we always use it."

Timothy opened his eyes.

"No! I wish my Uncle George could hear you. He's head of the business and very gloomy. It would cheer him up. Aristocratic bridesmaid confesses that she always washes 'the smalls' in Munster."

Ann laughed.

"Aren't you silly."

They had been so deep in what they were saying they had forgotten the time. They were startled by the Marchioness's voice.

"Oh, here you are Timothy, you bad boy. We've been looking for you everywhere. It's time you made your speech. Mona's going to cut the cake." Then she looked at Ann. "And you too, dear. All the other bridesmaids are round Mona." Her voice was quite kind. But as she moved away

Ann flushed. There had been no spoken reproof but it was implied. Ann too read into what had not been said.

"You may be acting bridesmaid for the afternoon but that's no reason why you should sit about in corners with the best man."

Timothy was unabashed. He put his hand under Ann's elbow and together they slid off the table. He did not let go of her arm but steered her through the guests.

"Can I have a lot of dances tonight, Sally?"

Ann had forgotten the talk in the car going to the church.

"Tonight! Where?"

"The bridesmaids' hop. At the Savoy."

"Oh! That. Well I can't go."

He stood still.

"Of course you're going. All eight of you are booked. I'm putting in to drive you up."

"I can't go. Really I can't."

"Why?"

Ann searched for a good reason.

"I've got to go home."

"But aren't your people staying in London?"

"Yes."

"Well then, what's the trouble. You can go home after the dance."

"No. I must go after the wedding."

"I never heard such talk. I'll put Mona onto you."

Timothy did not get a chance to catch Mona alone until after the speeches and cake-cutting. Then he succeeded in engineering himself next to her.

"A very pretty speech you made," said Mona.

Timothy nodded.

"No question about it, the fellow ought to be in parliament. Listen, duckie. Before you go into the night with that unspeakable cad you've married would you do a last good deed?"

Mona took a piece of wedding cake from a passing tray. "Course."

"Sally won't dance tonight. Would you influence her to snap out of such foolishness?"

"Sally!" Mona looked thoughtfully at her piece of cake. "Have you taken a fancy to her?"

"Maybe."

Mona raised her eyes to his.

"Well, I wouldn't. I mean don't go falling for her properly. You'll be in one hell of a mess if you do."

"Why?"

"I can't explain. But honestly it wouldn't work."

Timothy eyed her with a question-mark brow.

"Very cryptic these young brides are. I'm not asking to marry the girl. Only to dance with her. Be a pal."

"I'm not sure if it is being a pal."

"Now don't go all matronly. You've only been married five minutes. Nip off and tell her she's going to the Savoy and I'm driving her there."

Mona ate the last crumb of her cake while she considered. "All right. But I'm not sure it's a good deed."

"There," said Manners. "Just take a look at yourself."

Ann spun round to face the long glass. It was very nice what she saw. She caught her breath with pleasure. A little tight bodice, the waistline held in with silver and blue cascades of ribbon. The skirt was practically a crinoline. She turned back to Manners.

"Are you sure her ladyship meant me to wear this?"

"That's right." Manners knelt to adjust the lining of the skirt. "'Put her in my pink, Manners,' she said. 'It'll suit her and there's those silver shoes that were too small for me she can wear with it.'"

"Fancy her thinking of all that for me on her wedding day."

"Full of it she was when I was dressing her to go away. 'Isn't it lucky, Manners,' she said,' that you're not joining me till tomorrow.' You can see she's all right."

"She is kind."

"She is that." Manners's voice was affectionate. "Never hear her say an unkind thing. Sit down by the dressing-table, dear, while I just turn your curls over my finger."

Ann sat and looked at Manners in the glass.

"Everyone has been so nice to me. Or at least nearly everyone."

"Who hasn't?"

Ann did not answer directly.

"Is Miss Bolt very fond of Sir Timothy Munster?"

Manners made a disparaging sound.

"Her! Might have known it would have been. Yes. They were brought up together. It was kind of understood if you understand me. But when Sir Timothy grew up he had different ideas."

"You mean he's fond of somebody else?"

"No. Doesn't take to anyone in particular. Full of his business he is. He's not for settling down. When he does it might be Miss Cora after all. You never know." Manners hesitated. "He's driving you up isn't he?"

"Yes."

"Well you want to take him with a pinch of salt. You won't be used to his kind. He's a nice gentleman but friendly with all. Upset a lot of young ladies he has."

Ann flushed.

"He wouldn't upset me. I mean of course after tonight I shan't see him again."

"No, that's right." Manners fixed the last curl. She went over to a cupboard and took out an ermine coat. "Here's the coat you're to wear."

"Oh, no! It's ermine. I might lose it."

"No you won't. The address of the furriers is on the lining. Lady Mona, or rather her ladyship I should say now, said you were to leave it there for her. The other things you can just post back to me." She helped Ann into the coat.

"Gosh," said Ann. "Ermine! I never thought I'd wear it."

"Never know what's coming to us." Manners picked up a silver bag. "Here's your bag. I've packed your own in the box with your things, it's in Sir Timothy's car. The money in this is for you with her ladyship's love."

Ann opened the bag and saw folded in a pocket a five-pound note. She had never owned a five-pound note. She had to unfold it to see what it was. It crackled. It looked gloriously rich. She folded it again and handed it to Manners.

"Will you thank her. Tell her I was grateful, but if she didn't mind I'd rather not. Today has been lovely, something I'll never forget. I don't want it mixed up with tips."

Manners took the note. She hesitated. Then she put it on the dressing-table.

"There's some silver in the purse. You must have some on you for the cloakroom and that. You can return it to her ladyship later if you like. I'd meant to put it in your bag anyhow."

Ann took a last look round the room. She tried to photograph it so that always when things were drab she could call it back. She didn't envy Mona. Didn't want to spend her life being dressed by a maid. But it was the first time she had known how it feels to be perfectly turned out all over. It was the first time she had known how it feels to be thought a somebody. The first time she had known how it feels to glow in your heart because you are dancing with a special man.

She turned and flung her arms round Manners.

"Goodbye, Manners. You have been so kind."

Manners stood looking down the passage after Ann. Then came back into the bedroom. She picked up the five-pound note.

"Poor little girl," she thought. "Her ladyship meant all right. But I'd bet there'll be many a wet pillow before she's through."

CHAPTER FOUR

Bunny sat in the kitchen while his mother cooked. In front of him was a saucer of water. Floating in the water were flower transfers. His head was bent over a scrapbook. With a handkerchief he was dabbing a transfer dry. In his excitement he breathed heavily through his nose.

"Mum, it's bluebells. I bet this one comes out well." Alice looked across from her stove. She smiled at the absorption in every line of him.

"That'll be something nice to show Ann when she gets in. It was a good idea of hers buying you those."

"Yes." Bunny slowly slid the sodden paper from the transfer. "Look, Mum. It's perfect."

Alice left the gravy she was making. She leant over his shoulder.

"Splendid, son. Ann'll like that."

He nodded.

"I wish she'd come home."

Alice looked up at the clock. "Won't be long now. Be ready for her supper. She'll do with something warm in her on a night like this." She went back to the stove. Suddenly she raised her head. "Was that the bell, Bunny?"

Bunny pushed a transfer under the water.

"Yes. Must be a new lodger."

"Haven't room for any more. I wonder if your father heard it." They both listened. Then as a door opened and there were steps on the stairs they went on with what they were doing. "That's the best of having been trained a chemist. No matter what you're doing you seem to hear bells."

Alfred opened the door.

"It's a telegram."

"For us?"

He nodded.

"Well, open it."

He gingerly pulled up the flap. Alice watched him nervously. He smiled at her.

"Hate the things. Don't you?" He opened the form. Then he whistled. "Hark to this. 'Am dancing tonight. Will not be home till late. Put key usual place. Ann!'" Alice stopped stirring.

"Dancing tonight! She can't be. Why she had on that dress cousin Jane gave her and those thick shoes I made her buy."

Alfred went into the passage and called out to the telegraph boy that there was no answer. He came back. "Funny. Wonder who she's dancing with?"

Alice held out her hand.

"Let's see it."

He passed it over.

"You can't see more than I've read."

"Oh! Look." She came to him so he could read with her. "See where it's sent off from. Lewes."

"That's in Sussex," said Bunny.

"I know." Alice spoke excitedly. "That's where that big wedding was today. She said Miss Briggs was going down to do the bride's face. Must have sent her instead."

Alfred laughed, looking at Bunny.

"Your mum would have made a good detective." He turned back to Alice. "Now tell us who she's dancing with?"

They all loved Alice's romances.

Bunny got up.

"Go on, Mum."

"Well," Alice stirred a moment while she thought. "After the wedding there's going to be a dance. And Ann made the bride look so lovely this afternoon that her mother, that's the Marchioness of Manton said, 'You must make up my face for tonight, Miss Lane.'"

"But she said she was going to dance," Bunny objected.

Alice held up her hand.

"One minute, son. I'm coming to that. And while she was in the house a royal prince saw her and he said 'Lovely creature, who are you?'"

"You forget she has on cousin Jane's old frock," Alfred pointed out.

"You wait. And she said in her saucy way 'I'm the Lady Ann Vere de Vere,' and he said 'Will you dance with me at the ball tonight?' And she said 'These are all the clothes I have.' And he said 'You look perfect. I never want to see you in anything else.'"

Alfred laughed.

"He was crackers if he said that."

"So Ann is staying to the dance."

"And," said Bunny "then she'll marry the prince and live happily ever afterwards."

"Almost always happily," Alice went back to her gravy.

"I think if you're always happy you might get tired of it."

Alfred put his arm round her and gave her a squeeze.

"Not had much chance to find out have you, old dear?" Then he added as an afterthought, "Whoever she's dancing with I hope she doesn't forget the time of her last bus home."

"And so," said Timothy not taking his eyes off the road ahead, "You won't talk about yourself."

Ann hesitated.

"I'm not meaning to be mysterious. If you knew you'd understand."

"Right, we'll leave it there. He's such a curious boy. He was like that as a child." His voice took a more serious note. "It's Mona's fault."

"Why?"

"She made you sound so unattainable." He took a hand off the wheel and laid it on her knee a second. "All right, duckie. Be what you like. An international spy, or a foreign royalty in disguise as long as you go on being 'Just Sally.'"

She caught her breath. It was on the tip of her tongue to say I'm not even that. I'm Ann. He gave her a quick look.

"No, don't stop me. Driving with you rolled up in your furs, with the lights of London ahead seems to have made me a bit drunk. It's such fun. Tonight's ours and there's always tomorrow. Oh, Sally, have you ever thought what a lot of amusing things there are to do if you do them in the right company?"

Ann snuggled into the ermine coat. Inside its warmth she felt cut off from Ann Lane. Almost she could believe that she was different. That for her there was a tomorrow like this. A tomorrow with no Maison Pertinax. A tomorrow with a lot of amusing things to do in the right company.

"You're tired," he said gently. "How about ten minutes shuteye. You'll need your health and strength if you're going to dance with me."

The car turned out of the Strand, under the arch and drew up at the entrance to the Savoy. Ann woke up with a jump. She blinked at Timothy.

"Have I been asleep?"

"You certainly have. Your head rolled very pleasantly on to my shoulder. Nice it was. Jump out, duckie."

Ann got out. She looked rather nervously at the uniformed man holding open the door for her. She glanced back at Timothy.

"Aren't you coming? I'd rather wait for you."

"You hop in and powder your nose. Just got to arrange about parking the car."

Ann turned obediently, when she remembered her box of clothes.

"Oh, my box."

He looked at it where it lay on the back seat.

"Don't want that now, do you? I'll drive you home."

"No." Not waiting for the man she opened the back of the car. "I must have it. I mean I think I'll want something out of it."

Timothy leant back and put a hand on her shoulder.

"All right, sweet. Anything you say." He held up a finger to the man. "Give this to a page and see it's taken to the ladies' room."

The Savoy to Ann was the place where the dance music on the wireless came from. Though she had often listened to it she had never bothered to wonder what the place was like where it came from. The reality seemed crushingly grand. Ann needed all her ermine and pink tulle to take herself across the lounge. "If only," she thought, "I wasn't alone."

The attendant in the cloakroom gave her a ticket for her box and coat. Standing before a mirror she folded the ticket and put it in her bag. There was an odd rather sad little smile on her face as she did it. Ticket one hundred and ten. When the attendant got that back a dream would be over. Bridesmaid Sally would disappear.

Looking back on the evening afterwards Ann could only remember bits. There were cocktails first at a little table on the floor just above the restaurant. From where she sat she could see right across the dining-room. Such a lot of people, and so smart.

Their table, when they got to it, was specially decorated. Lovely bowls of roses. People turned to stare as they filed in. They whispered "There are the bridesmaids and ushers from the Manton wedding."

Ann sat on one side of Timothy, Cora on the other. Cora had a great deal to say it seemed. Timothy's back was often turned to Ann. She found herself involved in long talks with an almost white haired young man on her left. It was not so much talk as conversation pieces by the young man. Directly Ann turned towards him he said "Hunt?" and when she said "No," he said "Should." After that he evidently thought it his duty to educate her. Quite unmoved by her ignorance he launched into a long description of a day's hunting. She could not possibly enter a conversation made up of "There's wire there. Fellow goes in for grouse. Shockin' unsportin'. Well, we come out through a gap and—" it flowed on unceasingly. Ann only had to smile and keep up an interested "Yes."

At the end of dinner they danced.

"Might as well tread the light and fairy," said the hunting young man.

Ann glanced at Timothy. He seemed to be talking to someone across the table. Unwillingly she turned to say "Yes." Timothy caught her wrist.

"Half a second, duckie. This is ours, remember."

"Oh I say—" The hunting young man protested. "Have a heart."

Timothy laughed.

"I have. That's why."

Cora was making up her lips. Her eyes were on her mirror. She made no sign that she had heard the conversation. But Ann saw her jawbone move as if she were setting her mouth in a grim line.

"That's the worst of dinner parties," said Timothy, steering her through the tables to the dance floor. "Always having to talk to both sides of you."

Ann wanted most dreadfully to make him talk about Cora. She knew it was not her business but she felt she must hear how he really felt about her. Was Manners right? Was all the being fond on her side?

"I expect Miss Bolt was being very interesting," she said childishly.

He tucked his arm round her waist. The orchestra was playing "Oh Mama." The floor was crowded. There was no room for anything but rhythmic walking. He looked down into her eyes.

"I'm sure she doesn't want to be called Miss Bolt. Cora's the name. She can't be dull. Most amusin' girl I know. She was being a scream about the wedding."

Ann sighed. Why was it some people could be permanently amusing. She was never short of conversation, but she was hardly ever funny.

"It's nice to make people laugh."

He paused.

"Aren't you a comic. It's all right at dinner and times like that. But I wouldn't want it for long."

"Oh." Their feet moved on again. Ann's much lighter to match her heart which suddenly felt as if it had been blown up like a penny balloon.

The first cabaret came on after that. Ann enjoyed it. She liked seeing the dancing floor rise to form a stage. There were some very clever tumblers, a man and woman who danced, and two Frenchmen with some performing poodles.

Ann, engrossed in the cabaret, never noticed Timothy. She was quite unconscious that his eyes were not on the stage, but fixed on her face. But Cora noticed, and there were angry lines round her mouth. Some of the others noticed Cora. There was a lot of nudging round the table. "Sally better watch her step. If she's not careful Cora will give her a nasty bite."

"Shall we step again, Sally?" Timothy said as the curtains swung together, hiding the variety artistes, and the stage sank back to its humble job of dancefloor.

Ann got up. She felt quite ridiculously happy. It was all being such fun. The glamour of the evening had shut her in as if she were cut off from the world. Just for this one evening the fairytale was true. Timothy put his arm round her to dance.

"When am I going to see you again?"

Ann raised startled eyes to his. She felt as if a door into her fairyland had been pushed open. A cold blast had blown in.

"Oh—I don't know."

"How about tomorrow night?"

"Not tomorrow."

"Well, when? Where are you staying? The Berkeley, aren't you?"

Ann could not bear to he to him, but the Berkeley did seem a way out. She gave a faint nod.

"Good." He steered her dexterously between two couples. "I'll give you a ring in the morning. Have the engagement book ready. You may not know it, but you and I are going to see a lot of each other."

Ann felt a lump in her throat. She wanted to make one of her ordinary cheeky offhand retorts. Somehow she couldn't.

She found herself wishing no desperately that it was true. She wriggled free of his arm.

"Sorry." She spoke in a small voice. "I'm tired. Let's sit down."

The rest of the party were still at the table. They were gossiping and smoking.

"My word," said Primrose. "There's a type. Look at that girl, isn't she terrific?"

Her partner looked in the direction of her eyes.

"I bet she's taking it out of sugar daddy."

The hunting young man turned round to look.

"Rather luscious."

His partner looked over her shoulder.

"Seems interested in Sally."

Ann grew cold. She tried to attend to what Timothy was saying, but her ears were strained to catch the comments of the rest of the table.

"Seems uncommon taken with someone at our table," the hunting young man agreed.

"It's you and Sally, Timothy," one of the others remarked. "I thought she was going to swoon with excitement when you walked by."

Cora gave Sally a look. She caught her slowly flushing.

"Do you know her?"

Ann shook her head.

"I haven't seen her."

"Well, turn and have a look."

Ann turned. Four tables away Iris sat with a bibulous old man. Iris' eyes, fixed on Ann, were goggling with amazement. Ann kept her eyes blank. She did not allow one gleam of recognition to show in them. She turned back casually to Cora.

"I believe I have seen her somewhere."

"She seemed to know you all right."

Timothy looked at Cora in surprise.

"Really, duckie, as the most photographed queen of the muck press, you must have got used to being stared at. Why shouldn't Sally?"

Cora shrugged her shoulders and dropped the subject. But her eyes on Ann were calculating.

Ann, while managing to give a semblance of joining in with the general conversation, racked her brains for her best way of escape. She dare not leave now. Iris' unblinking stare told her that at her first move to the cloakroom she would be after her. There was only one thing for it. The party had decided to stay till after the second cabaret. It meant staying far later than Ann had intended. But it would give her a chance to slip out in the dark. To the party it would seem the usual "I must powder my nose." With luck Iris wouldn't see her go at all.

It worked. The lights had barely dimmed for the cabaret to start when Ann got up. She was not next to Timothy. She was between two cousins of Mona's.

"Shan't be a minute," she whispered.

No one else noticed she had gone. In a second she was up the steps. In another she was holding out number 110 to the cloakroom attendant. Then suddenly as she was being helped into her coat a thought struck her. She couldn't quite leave Timothy like that. She asked for a piece of paper. She wrote:

"I've got a headache and have gone home. Thank you for everything. Goodbye, Sally."

The Savoy staff made everything easy. Yes, of course they knew Sir Timothy. Yes, of course, they would give him the note. A taxi? Of course. Almost before she had gathered her wits together Ann, with her box on the floor at her feet, was driving out into the Strand.

As the lights went up after the cabaret it was noticed Sally had not come back.

"One of the girls better see she's all right," Timothy suggested.

Primrose got up to go, but at that moment the note arrived.

"She's gone home," Timothy said briefly. "Got a head-ache. If it comes to that, about time we all went."

Cora played with her cigarette.

"Because you've not further interest in the evening, it doesn't follow that we haven't."

Jane got up.

"Timothy's quite right. I don't know about you, Cora, but I'm for hitting the hay. I'm tired as a dog."

Iris had noticed with disgust that Ann had gone. She would have to wait till the morning now to find out how she came to be mixed up with such exalted people. All the same, there was a chance she might hear something tonight. She gave her sugar daddy an affectionate pat.

"Must do something about my nose. Shan't be long."

Cora, while putting on her coat, saw Iris come into the cloakroom. She followed her over to one of the dress-ing-tables. She gave her a smile.

"You know Sally Groot, don't you?"

"Now what's this?" thought Iris. "Her sort doesn't talk to my sort for nothing. And who the hell is Sally Groot?"

"No." She powdered her nose. "Don't think so. Why?"

"I thought you looked as though you knew her. She was at our table tonight. Wearing rose colour."

"Strewth!" thought Iris. "What's Ann up to?" But her face expressed nothing at all.

"No." She used her lipstick carefully. "I'm just the staring kind. One of nature's rubbernecks." She turned. "So long."

Cora stood looking after her. What was all this mystery? She picked up her bag and went into the lounge. "I'll find out," she resolved. "Can't have that blasted girl snooping Timothy."

Iris on her way back to the ballroom saw Cora and the rest of the party leave the hotel. She gave a pleased smile at Cora's back.

"You go home to bed and bad dreams to you Miss Nosey Parker."

As Ann's taxi stopped the lights sprang up in the house.

"There's Ann," said Alice, hustling into her dressing-gown. "Glad whoever it is has had the sense to drive her home."

Alfred got out of bed.

"I'll just come down a minute to hear what she's been up to."

"There's Ann," thought Nurse. "I think I'll just slip down and tell her she's a dirty stop-out. Nothing like having a good laugh."

"There's Miss Ann," thought Thomas Bloom, the boarder in the small front room. "I must just slip into the passage and hear what's happened to her. Not at all like her, this stopping out late."

Miss Maggie Dean, a schoolteacher who boarded in the largest of the bedrooms, heard Ann's key in the lock. She sat up in bed and switched on the light. She clicked her tongue as she saw the time.

"My word, that girl's late." She got out of bed and opened her door a crack.

Oswald Perkins, the clerk who had the top room at the back, was only just in himself. He heard Ann's key with a grin.

"Not the only one to come in with the milk," he thought. He put on his coat again. It was dull coming back to a dark house. He'd just slip down and ask her if she's had a good time.

The key was under the scraper. Ann found it and put it in the lock. It was stiff to turn; it needed both hands. She put down her box. Then softly, so as to wake no one, she picked it up again, opened the door and walked in.

Alfred and Alice were in the hall. Oswald Perkins had reached the top of the stairs. Nurse was leaning over the upper landing banister, Mr. Bloom over the one on the first floor. Alfred had switched on the hall lights. It was seldom a girl made a more startling entrance than Ann. The amazed gasp from everybody made Miss Dean draw her dressing-gown tight round her and scurry out on to the landing.

Ann, tired physically and mentally, had forgotten for the moment how she looked. She just knew that it was terribly nice to find Alice and Alfred up: She never noticed the others.

"Oh, mum and dad, you ought to be in bed."

"What's happened, dear?" said Alice, staring at the ermine coat.

Ann suddenly remembered. She laughed. She gave the coat a pat.

"Oh, this. It's all right. Go on up, both of you. I've such a lot to tell you."

Silently the boarders slipped back to their rooms.

"Phew!" thought Oswald Perkins sympathetically. "I wouldn't be her for a lot. Those togs will take some explaining."

"Really!" Miss Dean took off her dressing-gown. "What sort of a house is this? And I always thought her such a nice girl."

Nurse got back into bed, shaking with laughter. "Oh, this! It's all right." She repeated to herself: "That's the way to talk of an ermine coat."

Mr. Bloom blinked in a puzzled manner at his little room.

"It must be all right," he consoled himself. "Anything Miss Ann does must be all right. But—"

Ann had settled down on the end of her mother's bed. Without a word of interruption she told her story from beginning to end. There was just one thing she left out. She never mentioned Timothy.

"Oh, my goodness," said Alice. "What a thrill. There's such a lot I want to ask."

Alfred got up and put his arm round Ann.

"It'll have to wait, then. She's tired, and she's got to work in the morning."

It was those words Ann heard as she took off Mona's clothes. She had hung up the frock and coat. She had taken off the last of the underthings. They lay in a little white satin circle round her feet. She had a sudden feeling she was going to cry. Despising such weakness, she pushed the things to one side and savagely pulled on her own pyjamas.

"No good snivelling," she told herself fiercely. "Dad's right, you've got to work tomorrow."

CHAPTER FIVE

IT WAS five minutes past nine when Ann came into the Maison Pertinax the next morning. Lila's eyes snapped with pleasure. Ann late. It was the sort of opportunity for which she had been waiting.

"Good morning." She looked ostentatiously at the clock. "Five past nine. It's very inconsiderate to be late with Miss Briggs away."

"Sorry," said Ann, and passed on to the stairs. Lila was not going to let her go so easily.

"Just because Mr. Pert let you take Miss Brigg's place yesterday, that's no reason why you should think you can take liberties today."

Ann paused.

"I'm sorry. I had to call at a shop on the way. It didn't open till nine."

"I doubt if Mr. Pert would think shopping in his time quite what he paid you for."

Ann flushed. She couldn't explain. Couldn't turn round and say, "I wasn't shopping. I was leaving a borrowed ermine coat at a furrier's." All the same, Lila was making too much fuss. She had never been late before. There was no need to nag the first time it happened. Besides, she was in no mood for Lila this morning. She just wanted to be left alone. Left to work and work until she had forgotten about yesterday and felt just Ann Lane again. She came back to the desk.

"Look here, I am late; I've admitted it. You're not making me any earlier by keeping me talking here. You always threaten what Mr. Pert will say. Well, why don't you report me? Tell Mr. Pert."

Lila looked down at the ledger in front of her. Telling Mr. Pert was the one thing she did not want to do. If she told him he would probably say "Five minutes late! Dear, dear. Tell her she must be punctual in future." And forget all about it. As a threat Mr. Pert was grand. In actual fact he was a letdown.

"I'll let you off this time, but don't let me have to complain again. Now, please hurry."

Ann hesitated. It was on the tip of her tongue to tell Lila she didn't want her leniency. That she'd go to Mr. Pert herself. Good sense won, however. Inwardly boiling, she went downstairs.

Lila looked after her, loathing her more than ever. There was something about Ann. Her ability to think for herself, her refusal to eat humble pie. "Upset the whole shop before she's through," she muttered as she went back to sorting the day's appointments.

Ann passed most of the other girls on the stairs. "Hullo, Ann. Did you see anything of the wedding?" asked Kitty.

Biddy held her by the arm.

"What's the man like she's marrying?"

Agnes peered near-sightedly at her through her glasses.

"I don't suppose you saw him, did you?"

"Sure, and she did then," said Norah. "You wouldn't be at a wedding and not catch sight of the bridegroom, would you now?"

June's head appeared at the bottom of the stairs.

"What did Lady Mona wear? She looked lovely in her pictures this morning." She sighed. "So slim."

"Girls"—Lila came to the top of the stairs—"it's ten past nine. Really, Ann, I should have thought you'd caused enough trouble being late without adding to it by gossiping on the stairs."

With the rudest faces at Lila's back the girls trooped up. Betty, who was last, whispered, "Were you given any wedding cake?" And on getting Ann's nod went up looking as pleased as if she had eaten the cake herself.

Ann, unbuttoning her coat as she went, hurried to the cloakroom. Sitting on the table obviously waiting for her were Iris and Connie.

"Well, well!" said Iris. "And how is Miss Groot this morning?"

Ann stood still and stared at her. She had planned how to deal with Iris. She would question her, of course, and when she did she would look blank. People often looked like each other. She would laugh and say, "Me at the Manton bridesmaids' party! Are you mad? I must have a double." But this calling her Sally Groot took the wind out of her sails.

"Now look here." Iris got off the table and put her arm through Ann's. "There's no need to look scared. Connie and me are good sports. We won't give you away. But you've got to tell us who you are; fair's fair."

"That's right," Connie agreed. "You see, us girls can hold our tongues. We need to, or goodness knows where we'd be."

"Connie, Iris," called Lila, "what are you up to?"

"Sorry," Iris sniffed. "My node is bleeding and Connie's puddin' a key down my back."

Lila made an annoyed clicking.

"Well, come up as soon as possible."

"Yes," Iris agreed. They listened to Lila's departing footsteps. "Old cat! Now, come on, Ann."

"I can't explain now." Ann hurried into her overall. "I'm already late. She's furious."

Connie sighed.

"Sour puss. I'd like to bash her face in." Iris grabbed hold of Connie.

"Come on. Let's dash through our work, then we can slip into Ann's cubicle and hear."

"You can't unless I'm through," said Ann. "You forget Minnie Briggs is away and I'm doing double."

Iris was halfway to the door.

"No good taking that tone, old dear. You want to make a friend of me. I'm lovely when I'm on your side, but a bagful of trouble when I'm on the other."

Ann's chin shot up.

"No one's ever scared me yet, and they aren't going to start now, Iris. It's perfectly true I was at the party last night, and I know you saw me, and somehow found out I was pretending to be Sally Groot, but I've done nothing to be ashamed of, and neither you nor anybody else can bully me. Now I'll go up. If I'm through in time I'll tell you all about it, but because I want to and not because you've made me."

By lightning work Ann was just finished when Iris and Connie came in. Iris looked round.

"Through?"

"All but putting this tray straight."

Iris lay down on the couch.

"Let Connie do it; you can do something to my face, and then if Nosey P comes in I'll say I mucked it up when my nose bled."

Ann's face expressed distaste.

"I hate the sight of her, but I don't like lying to her. If she comes in we're gossiping, and that's that."

Ann told a shortened account of yesterday's doings; Iris and Connie were spellbound.

"Bridesmaid with Lady Primrose and Lady Jane!" gasped Connie.

"They were awfully nice," said Ann; "in fact, I liked them all except Miss Bolt."

Iris wriggled on the couch.

"There's just one word for that lady, and it begins with a B."

"Go on, Ann." Connie gave the make-up tray a final flick with the duster. "What happened after the wedding?"

Ann skipped the part in the vestry, the kiss and the few words with Cora.

"At the reception Lady Mona told Sir Timothy Munster he must look after me."

Iris sighed.

"There are fairies at the bottom of your garden."

"And he was awfully kind, and thinking I was Sally Groot, he said he'd motor me up to town for the bridesmaids' party, and of course I was in an awful stew. I said I couldn't and all that, but he went to Lady Mona, and she fixed it, and she lent me her clothes to wear."

Iris turned to Connie.

"You should have seen her. Talk of the upper ten! She looked in the last two. What's he like, Ann?"

Ann flushed and stooped over her tray, pretending to wipe off a speck of powder.

"Oh, I don't know."

Iris sat up.

"Come off it. He was all over you. You know how he looked; I told you, Connie."

Ann's heart missed a beat.

"He wasn't. I think it was just Lady Mona asked him to be kind."

"Oh, yeah!" Iris combed her platinum curls. "I know that look on a man's face. It never came because he was being kind to anyone."

"Us girls," Connie explained, "are very good at knowing looks on men's faces."

Iris turned round.

"Besides, what else upset the Honourable Cora Bolt?"

Ann looked up.

"Do you know her?"

"Only by her pictures. And seeing her around. But she spoke to me. Very nosey about you."

Ann heard the cloakroom conversation. She smoothed the rug where Iris had made a dent.

"She needn't worry. I'll never see him again."

"Iris and Connie!" Lila's voice came shrilly up the corridor.

Back in their cubicles, Connie put her head round Iris's curtain.

"Did you hear that? Do you know I think she's fallen for him."

"Think!" Iris's face expressed volumes. "You ought to have seen her face last night, then you'd have known. Tell you what. I think the poor little cow needs friends."

Connie blinked.

"What's the matter with us?"

Iris powdered her nose.

"That's right. Knowing men as we do, we're just the ones to see her through." Lila's bell rang sharply three times. "Blast, there's my old Countess. If I was aristocracy you'd never find me making a hairdresser's appointment at this time."

In a house like the Lanes' what concerned one concerned all. Naturally the Lanes disliked having boarders; but since they had to be they accepted them more or less as members of the family. Their coming had meant sacrifices. Ann gave up her large room over her parents to Miss Dean and took to the little top front room which had been a boxroom. Bunny had to give up his room over the bathroom to Nurse, and slept in the small back room under Oswald Perkins.

Alice suffered most. Though wild horses would not have dragged from her that she minded at all. If the others grumbled she always said:

"I like having them. It's company."

Inside she detested it. Not that she minded the boarders personally; she didn't. Once they were in the house she treated them as some of her family. But she hated not having the house to herself. She was proud of her home. It was, of course, old fashioned, and you couldn't keep it warm in the winter, but having three floors gave a nice feeling of space. She would never forget the day she first saw it. It was a week after the day she had told Alfred Ann was on the way, and they'd have to have a bigger place.

"Come for a walk," Alfred had said.

They had walked up the King's Road and turned off and presently came to Number 95 Anchor Street. Alfred had taken a key out of his pocket. He had unlocked the front door. He had taken her all over the house. Then down in the hall he had held her by the shoulders.

"How's that for a place to bring up a family?"

How excited she had been.

"Not really? Are you sure you can afford it?"

Alfred had been doing well, then. There had been a nice secure feeling about the way he had said "quite."

It wasn't only having strangers in the house Alice minded. It was the work it gave to Alfred. It had been bad enough when the flats had come and each year he had done worse. Of course she had minded. It had been dreadful the day he had told her he had to sell the shop. She hadn't liked to think of him with nothing to do because she knew he'd hate it. But by having something to do she had never even pictured the things he did do. He'd always looked so smart. He'd looked like a chemist who only wasn't a doctor because he couldn't pay the fees. And now! Carrying up breakfast trays. Scrubbing out the kitchen. Doing the stairs. Paraffining the bath. He had even wanted to do the steps and the outside brass. She had struck there. He couldn't see why she had cried. But since it made her cry he gave in. He said it worried him thinking she was out there in the cold, but if someone had to be upset better him than her.

Accepting the boarders as family gave them certain rights. They could worry if Bunny looked peaky; they could admire Ann's clothes; they could bring in an evening paper for Alfred to save him buying one. But they couldn't criticise. If there was any criticising to be done Alice could manage it without help. But in the days which followed the wedding she had a job to stall it off. Not that any of them actually said anything unkind, but they did give the effect that the little they did say was only half what they would like to.

Ann did not help. Only four people knew what had happened. Only two knew about Timothy. Alice and Alfred, while appreciating that a thing like the wedding happening to a girl upsets her, could see no reason why after a couple of days she wasn't herself again. Iris and Connie never bothered to wonder how Ann was feeling. They treated her rather as Mona and Manners had treated her while they were dressing her. A doll that they owned and could do what they liked with.

Ann was feeling anything but all right. She had never guessed how much missing people could hurt. It seemed impossible that she could go on being so silly about a person she had only met once. But she could. She found his face and the way he said things coming between her and the world. Sometimes she would get up in the morning determined to snap out of such wool-gathering. Then something, perhaps a face in the street, or an advertisement for "Munster's Soap Flakes" on a hoarding, brought him back with such vividness that for a second she was dancing with him again, or sitting with him on the chest in the corner at the reception. Hearing him say "Quite right," "Just Sally," "I deserved that," or "When am I going to see you again?"

You can't have been the life and soul of a house full of inquisitive boarders without their noticing when you stop being the life and soul. Ann thought she was doing well. She cracked the same sort of jokes as before, laughed at the same things, tried to take the same interest in their doings. But the boarders knew the difference. At first they remarked on it to each other.

"Miss Ann hasn't seemed herself these last days," Mr. Bloom said to Miss Dean.

Miss Dean rather liked Mr. Bloom. She said he was "gentlemanly," by which she meant he didn't come in late and never took his bath at the time she liked hers.

"I've noticed it, too, I thought perhaps I'd ask her in for a little talk. Girls are glad to have someone to confide in."

Oswald Perkins met Nurse on the stairs.

"I say," he said awkwardly, "I think Ann's a bit off colour. You know what's wrong?"

Nurse nodded.

"What do you think? She's in love, my boy. I know that moony look."

"Really? Who with?"

"Ah!" Nurse wagged a finger at him. "If I knew I wouldn't tell. But as it happens I don't."

After a bit they stopped asking each other and asked Alice.

"Is Ann all right? Seems a bit down."

"I've been thinking Ann is not quite herself."

"Miss Ann is a bit depressed these days. I wish one could think of something to cheer her up."

Nurse was the only one who spoke out.

"Ann's fallen in love. You mark my words, my dear, there'll be orange blossom before Christmas."

To them all Alice was vague. "She's all right." And to Nurse, "Don't be silly." But she and Alfred worried.

"There is something up," Alfred said anxiously. "Seems as if the heart had gone out of her."

"That's what Nurse said." Alice paused to count the stitches in the sock she was knitting. "She says she's in love."

"Don't see how she can be," Alfred objected. "Who's she met? I don't suppose there's anybody up at her shop would interest her."

Alice laughed.

"There's only Mr. Pert!"

Alfred roared.

"That's good. I can't see her fancying the job of Mrs. Pert."

Alice laid down her knitting.

"Young Oswald Perkins is a bit taken with her. She's been out with him those few times."

"Not him." Alfred shook his head. "Not Ann's cup of tea. She's being kind, that's all." He hesitated. "You don't think, do you, that it's mixing with all those rich people? I mean that it's nothing to do with her falling in love. After all, seeing how they live and being one of them for a day is enough to upset a girl."

Alice's needles made an assured click-clack. She smiled up at Alfred.

"Our Ann! Don't you know your own daughter better than that?"

"All the same, it's since then she's been as she has," Alfred persisted.

Alice's head went up. Not even Alfred could suggest things like that.

"Well, been like what? A little down perhaps. Like as not we're all making mountains out of molehills. Maybe it's just a chill or something."

Alfred came across and gave her an affectionate pat.

"Old hen, aren't you, clucking round your chickens?"

Alice picked up her sock again.

"And I'll go on clucking if there's any chat about Ann."

Even Bunny noticed Ann was not quite as usual.

"Gosh, Ann's getting awfully slow," he grumbled. "That's two days she's promised to bring me some new transfers and forgot."

Alice was leaning over the stove. She straightened up. She said nothing for a minute. "This wouldn't do," she thought. "The weather being bad, Bunny was kept in. He looked forward to things. Ann knew that. Whatever her private troubles, no need to disappoint Bunny." Out loud she said:

"All right, son. You'll have them tomorrow. I'll remind her."

She came to Ann's room that night. Ann was supposed to be undressing, but she was sitting on her bed daydreaming.

"That's a nice way to get undressed," said Alice briskly.

Ann started up guiltily.

"Shan't be a minute."

"I hope not. Catching your death of cold." She sat down on the chair. "Don't forget those transfers for Bunny. It's two days you've forgotten them."

Ann flushed.

"I know. I am a beast, and he looks forward to them so. I can't think how I came to forget."

Alice smiled.

"I can. I wonder you remember anything these days."

Ann was at her dressing-table. She swung round.

"What d'you mean?"

"Don't look so fierce. But after all you have been wool-gathering a bit lately, haven't you?"

Ann had no idea she was any different to what she was usually. She knew how she felt inside, but nobody else knew that.

"No! You're imagining it."

"Then the whole house is," Alice retorted dryly.

Ann opened her eyes.

"Honest?"

Alice nodded. She got up. She put her arm round Ann.

"You've not been cross or anything like that. Just a bit 'bats in the belfry.' Besides, we've all had a little less of your sauce lately, and we miss it." She gave her a kiss. "Good night, darling. Sleep well."

Ann looked at the door as it closed behind her mother. Then she gave herself a shake and rapidly finished undressing. In bed she curled herself up in a tight ball and thought hard. So she was making an ass of herself, was she? "You are a maudlin fool," she told herself angrily. "Snap out of it. Wake up tomorrow and forget he's on the earth. You've got to start sometime, so why not now?"

Ann did manage better the next morning. It was Saturday, and that made her cheerful. It was a nice frosty morning, which had a cheering effect on the spirits.

At the shop she heard Minnie Briggs would be back on Monday. Hard for anybody to moon about with Minnie Briggs around.

Ann got a chance to say something to Iris and Connie she had been wanting to say ever since the morning after the wedding. It was while they were dressing the shop.

"I say," she slipped in Iris's cubicle, "you two will forget all about Sir Timothy, won't you?"

Iris put her head through Connie's curtain. She hissed through her teeth and gave her head a backward jerk. Connie knew the sign. She put down her duster and came in.

"Ann says," Iris remarked noncommittally, "will we forget all about Sir Timothy."

Connie blinked.

"Course not. Us girls never forget about men."

"You see," Ann explained, "I've got to forget. I mean, you see, he thinks I'm Miss Groot. He wouldn't want to know Ann Lane."

"Why not?" asked Iris. "Plenty of men as rich as him want to know Connie and me."

Ann could not say what she thought about that.

She just said lamely:

"Well, that's different."

Iris gave her basin edge a polish.

"Why? Men like girls like us. Someone to dance with, and all that."

Ann hesitated.

"I may be a fool, but I don't want that. At least not with him."

Iris nodded at Connie.

"Got it badly. What did I tell you?"

Connie nodded back.

"Poor little cow."

Iris paused in her polishing.

"Can't you go somewhere where you'd meet him? You know, like the Savoy."

Ann smiled.

"No, and I haven't the clothes if I could go."

Iris gave a final quick rub round with her polisher.

"You don't need always to look like you looked that night. Good thing, too. We girls would be ruined."

"No one can say Iris and me don't look nice." Connie put in. "And we hardly spend anything."

Ann fidgeted with her belt. Shop gossip had it that Iris and Connie never spent a penny of their own money on clothes.

"Even if I could raise a frock, I don't know anyone who goes to those sort of places, and honestly I don't want to. I just want to forget about him. It would be nice if you two would try and forget too."

Connie looked at Iris.

"Hasn't that old sap of yours got a boyfriend?"

"Ah!" said Iris, "that's an idea." She glanced consideringly at Ann. "Wonder if she could handle him?" Connie shrugged.

"If he's anything like your old sap I should think anyone could handle him. I'd take him on myself, only I've my hands full just now."

"It's not so much Percy is easy," Iris protested, "as I'm the sort of girl he likes."

Connie made a raspberry.

"Easy as milking a cow."

Iris folded her duster.

"Every girl can't milk a cow. I'd say she was one of them."

Ann had listened horror-struck to this conversation. A sickening vision came in front of her of herself at the Savoy with the sort of old man with whom she had seen Iris. Of course, if she allowed Iris to arrange it, fate would be sure to see it was a night when Timothy was there. Even the thought of Timothy seeing her with a man like that made her flush.

"I am—I mean I can't milk at all. Well, you know I wouldn't amuse your sort of friend."

This was unlucky. Iris and Connie looked at each other. "Anything queer about our friends?" asked Connie.

"Us girls are rather particular," said Iris.

"Oh, dear—" Ann, very red, tried to stammer her way back to safer ground. "No, of course not, but I just meant that, honestly, I'd rather be left to get over Timothy. Not that I'm in love with him—"

Iris and Connie exchanged a meaning look.

"Only I did like him rather. And I don't want to see him again. After all, he's not my sort. It wouldn't be any use."

"Use for what?" asked Iris.

Ann looked down at her fingers.

"I mean he wouldn't marry a girl like me."

"Marry!" Iris gasped.

Connie was so startled she nearly fell back into her cubicle.

Ann was still looking at her fingers. She didn't see the expressions on their faces.

"I don't mean he'd want to marry me either as Miss Groot or myself. But I do think I'd get fonder of him if I saw him again. So please—"

"Ann Lane," Lila's voice came rasping up the passage.

Connie faded into her own cubicle. Iris snatched at a clean glass-polisher.

"Here you are, dear," she said loudly. "And see you give it back."

Lila pulled the cubicle curtains.

"Really, Ann, what are you doing! I don't know what Mr. Pert would say if he heard you'd been caught gossiping at this time of day."

Iris was re-scrubbing the basin edge. She looked round in apparent surprise.

"Oh, but she wasn't. I'm too busy to gossip, anyway. She only came to borrow a clean cloth."

Lila moved on.

"Well, get on with your own work," she said sharply. "And don't let me have to complain again."

Connie's head came back into Iris's cubicle. She nodded in the direction of the departing Ann.

"That's the trouble of being a nice girl. You get funny ideas. Marriage!"

"What is it?" said Iris. "Never heard of it."

"It's what girls like us come to when the bloom's off." Iris grinned.

"My word, she's going to have a surprise all right! Think I'll ask Perce about his boyfriend. Time the poor little cow woke up."

"That's all right." Connie withdrew her head. "Lucky she knows girls like us to put her right."

It was always nice getting home on Saturdays. It was good to get in for lunch. Alice always managed to have something special. She said a girl who had to have a scratch lunch for five days out of seven needed something with a flavour to it on Saturdays and Sundays.

"That you, dear?" she called out as Ann opened the door. "I've your favourite lunch, so hurry up and wash." Ann pulled off her hat and looked round the kitchen door.

"Not toad-in-a-hole?"

Alice laughed and nodded.

"That's right, greedy. You hurry now."

By the time Ann came down Alfred was there. He had just finished serving the boarders' lunch. They had it in the big living-room. Alice kept the little back dining-room for the family.

"There's one thing I won't stand for," she had said, "and that's eating in a crowd. I don't mind putting up with the small room so long as we have somewhere on our own."

Her family at once felt the change in Ann. It was clear they had almost got their own Ann back. All the family jokes which had died while she was so distrait and depressed were brought out. Mr. Bloom and Miss Dean were the only boarders in to lunch. There was always a laugh when they were eating together. That Miss Dean approved of Mr. Bloom had not missed them. Alice said it was a shame to make fun of them, but she was easily led on to tell one of her fairy tales. It was about the food today. There was bubble and squeak as a vegetable. Alice had them all laughing at her imitation of Mr. Bloom saying he'd love to be a bubble to Miss Dean's squeak. There was fun, too, over Alfred. If he had to act waiter the only thing to do was to make a joke of it. Bunny gave orders as if he were a duke while the plates were being changed. Alfred played up to him, running with a napkin over his arm.

After lunch Ann helped her mother wash up. They said nothing over the dishes about last night's talk. But Ann knew from the way her mother hummed that she was feeling happy, and she never felt that if she thought one of them upset or anything like that.

Alfred was going to a football match with Mr. Bloom. There was a lot of laughing over it. Ann said it was a shame and if he had any tact he'd take Miss Dean. Ann wanted her mother to come for a walk with her, but Alice said she didn't feel like it, and then told Ann in a whisper that she was afraid if she did Bunny would want to come too. She didn't want to say "no" for fear of his getting to think too much about his health, but cold weather made him frisky, and then he came home all played out and would be no good for anything for perhaps a couple of days. But Ann was to go. A walk on a lovely day like this would do her good.

Ann did not go at once. She stayed a bit, talking to Bunny while he played with his new transfers. They were special ones of birds she had got him. He planned to make a frieze of them for his room.

"Just think, Ann, if I got enough they could go the whole way round. It would be like sleeping in a wood."

Ann looked at the assortment of robins, swallows, martins, and nightingales in front of him and smiled, but she answered soberly, "Yes, wouldn't it?" and added he was not to worry if it took all the transfers in London to finish the frieze; she'd get them for him.

She went out happy at the sight of his absorbed face. "What a beast I've been," she thought. "Just a few transfers and he's so pleased. Fancy me forgetting them."

She walked along the Embankment. She loved the power station. She stood looking at it. Its simple lines against the winter sky, the gulls, at a barge going by. Then she felt a touch on her arm. She turned round, startled. It was Timothy.

"You!" she gasped. In her "You" was all the pent-up feeling since the wedding. It was only one syllable, but it rang with gladness.

He took hold of her hands.

"My dear, Just Sally, where have you been? I've had six detectives, forty-eight bloodhounds and a gold stick in waiting searching for you."

She laughed.

"Aren't you silly?"

"Seriously." He took her arm and they walked on together. "I'd begun to think you were one of those mirage things they get on a desert. I began to think I'd only imagined I'd met you. Where have you been hiding, and why?"

"I haven't been."

"Oh, yes, you have. You've been 'wropped' in mystery. No good your denying it. First I go to The Berkeley, where I thought you were staying. 'Yes, you had been, but you'd left.' 'No, you'd not left an address.'"

Ann privately thanked her stars. How very lucky the Groot family had departed. She knew, of course, Sally was in a nursing home, but it would have been easy for her father and mother to have been about.

"Then I rang up the Castle," Timothy went on. "I got on to the Marchioness. She was very queer. She tried to pretend she didn't know who I meant."

"Oh, well—" said Ann. "I haven't seen her lately."

"My dear girl, you were a bridesmaid at the wedding, and the parents of the bride don't forget who the bridesmaids were about a week later."

"I expect she's been busy. One forgets things when one is."

"No, one doesn't. Not those sort of things. But that isn't all. Scenting a mystery, I rang up Hall, the lugubrious butler. 'Hall,' I said, 'that bridesmaid, Miss Sally. Could you let me have her address?'"

Ann pictured Hall faced with that question.

"What did he say?"

"That he didn't know it, but his voice was very queer. He sounded as if he wanted to say 'But I know where the body's buried.'"

"Poor Hall."

"But was Timothy, the pride of the Munsters, discouraged? He was not. I went to a girlfriend."

"Cora?"

"As a matter of fact, yes. 'Cora, my girl,' I said, have you seen anything of that frightful hag Sally?'"

Ann tried to sound casual.

"What did she say?"

"She was queerest of the lot. She said, 'I'd take a bet we shan't see her again.' And I said, 'Why?' and she said, 'There's something odd about her,' and I said, 'How?' and she said, 'I don't know, but I'll find out.'"

Ann said nothing. Her brain was revolving round a problem. Could she tell the truth? Would Lady Mona mind? She was positive that if she told him in confidence he would keep a secret. But supposing he didn't? Supposing he didn't? Supposing he thought the story of how the beauty specialist became a bridesmaid too good to keep to himself? Sadly she dismissed the idea. She could imagine nothing lovelier than this walk if only she might be herself. But it wasn't her secret. Unless Lady Mona said she might speak, she must go on pretending.

"Well," he said gently, "don't you think you might explain? There is a mystery, isn't there?"

"Yes."

"Are you going to tell me?"

"I can't. I would if I could, but I can't."

He stopped. He turned her towards him, looking as if he were going to say something. Instead he suddenly hailed a taxi.

"Tea," he said. "We'll have crumpets. Where shall we go?"

Ann hesitated. If she had a gleam of sense in her she knew she should say "No." But she couldn't. The temptation was too great. After all, one tea couldn't hurt. She looked down at her clothes.

"Somewhere very quiet. I'm not dressed for anywhere smart."

He looked at her brown coat and brown tricorne hat and slim nice-fitting shoes.

"Seems all right to me. But I'm all for quiet myself. We'll go to my flat."

Timothy had a flat in Hill Street. It was very modern, all chromium and leather. Going in the taxi, Ann had wondered about going alone to a man's flat. It seemed an Iris-and-Connie sort of thing to do. Against that Timothy had suggested it so naturally it was obviously the sort of thing he thought ordinary. Evidently his friends went to men's flats and thought nothing of it. To suggest she would rather go to a teashop seemed rude, as if she thought he might make love to her. Now she was in the flat she was very glad she had said nothing. It was so cosy and friendly, with the firelight blazing on the red leather. Timothy was so natural, no different now they were alone.

He drew two immense armchairs to the fire. He rang the bell. When the manservant appeared he said:

"Tea, and do you think you could lay your hands on some crumpets?"

The manservant could. By a chance he said they were having them themselves in the servants' dining-room.

Before tea Timothy was gay and rattled on covering a dozen subjects. Over tea he still chattered, but there was something serious behind it. The moment they had finished eating he rang to have the things cleared. When it was done and they were alone he lit a cigarette. He pulled his armchair close beside Ann's and linked his arm in hers.

"And now, duckie, for a serious talk. Do you know, Sally, that I've not been able to get you out of my mind?"

His voice was too serious for Ann to answer anything but sincerely.

"Then you must."

"Why?"

She found that difficult. She couldn't say "Because I'm not your sort," because anybody is the sort to be in a person's mind.

"Because you can't go on seeing me."

"But why?" He paused, tapping his cigarette on the ashtray. "I've got an idea why you faded out on me. Mona or somebody told you about me and Cora. That's right, isn't it?"

While he spoke Ann had felt suddenly hopeful. Had he guessed? If he had it released her from any promise. His idea of Cora took her by surprise.

"Cora," she repeated stupidly.

"Yes." He stretched his legs to the fire. "I think I'd like to tell you about that. I'm not a saint, I'd never pretend I was. But a lot of people think I've done the dirty on Cora and it's not true."

Ann had nothing to say. She made an encouraging sound to help him on.

"Our people, Cora's and mine, have got places side by side in Buckinghamshire. Cora and I were always about together as kids. I took her along huntin' when she went out on her first pony."

He paused. It gave Ann time to picture the scene and without jealousy to marvel at some people's luck. Cora on her first pony in her first little habit, while she at the same age was having a walk in the London streets for her only exercise.

"It was the same when I went to school. First minute I got back for the holidays I was on the telephone fixing to hunt or golf or what have you. They called us engaged, just as a joke, you know; we weren't more than five and seven when it started."

"And then you grew up?" said Ann, seeing it all.

"That's right. I don't know why, but I'd never taken the idea seriously. I mean you don't marry a person because you were friends as kids."

He stopped. Ann had a quick feeling of compassion for Cora. Timothy said you didn't marry a person because you were fond of them as kids. But suppose one of the kids went on being fond? Suppose she was more than fond, she was in love?

"How did Cora feel?"

Timothy made a restless movement as if he were shaking off something that wound itself round him and held him back.

"She feels much as I do, I expect." His voice was vague; there was something in it which stopped further questions.

Ann suddenly saw the clock. It was half-past five. She had not said she would be out to tea. Her mother might worry. She got up.

"I must go."

He got up too. He helped her into her coat.

"Right, I'll get a taxi. I'll take you home." It was not said casually. His inflexion on "I'll take you home" sounded determined. Ann faced him, buttoning her coat.

"No, I'm going alone." She hesitated, feeling for the right words. "I don't want you to know where I live."

He nodded.

"I've grasped that. But why?"

She fumbled with a button.

"Because of a promise to somebody else."

There was a sudden silence. It was as though Timothy held his breath. When he spoke he was deliberately offhand.

"Somebody you're marrying?"

She laughed.

"Goodness, no. Nothing like that."

"Then what? Nothing else could concern the question as to whether I'm seeing you again."

"Yes, it could. There's something I can't explain."

He shook his head.

"I'm not taking that. I like you, Sally, and I stand by the old Munster motto, 'Where you see a good thing freeze on to it.'"

She was glad the conversation had taken a lighter turn; it made it easier.

"Honestly, there is a good reason. I'd like to explain, but I can't till I see someone and ask if I can."

"When'll you see them?"

"Not just yet. They're away. But I will directly they come back."

He held her by the shoulders. He gave her a little shake.

"Is it going to be a matter of weeks or months, or what?"

Ann tried to remember if she had heard anything about Mona's honeymoon, but nothing came back to her.

"Weeks, I should think, but honestly I don't know."

He held her more firmly.

"If you hadn't such a ludicrously honest face I'd say you were fooling me. None of this makes sense, you know. It sounds as though you lived in the time of King Arthur. One of those women with names like Elaine who were held captive by a dragon or something."

Her face was suddenly wistful.

"The real reason is so dreadfully ordinary."

"Is it? I don't like it, but it seems I've got to lump it. But you don't leave this flat, my girl, until I have your promise that the day you see this skeleton in the cupboard, or whatever it is, you ring me up and fix a meeting."

"Even if they say I can't explain to you?"

"More than ever then. That's the kind of statement to get me going. You know, fighting with the old back against the wall."

Ann moved.

"I must go."

"All right, then. Give me your promise."

Ann looked up.

"I promise."

"Good." He took her arm and led her towards the lift. "You might as well promise, you know, for it's got to happen. I'm a stubborn man, and I'm telling you here and now I'm seeing a good deal of you later on."

CHAPTER SIX

IT WAS no good Ann pretending that she was not up in the clouds. Regardless of the boarders, she sang in her bath. Regardless of Lila and other pricks to the flesh, she danced through her work. She had seen Timothy again. She knew right down to the depths of her that he didn't give a damn if she was Sally or Ann. He wanted to see her again for herself. She remembered Manners' words, "You want to take him with a pinch of salt. You won't be used to his kind. He's a nice gentleman, but friendly with all. Upset a lot of young ladies, he has." But words like that meant nothing to her. Perhaps it had been true once. But everybody had to go round looking until they found the right person. Perhaps you had to upset a lot of people. Perhaps if you were as attractive as Timothy you couldn't help it.

It was hard not being able to see him now, but of course she could not let him take her about as Miss Sally Groot when at any minute the real Sally might come out of her nursing home. But she did not worry about the future. Lady

Mona would be sure to understand. She would probably see Timothy herself, or, if not, certainly let her tell him about the wedding.

In a way she was glad of an excuse not to see him. This delay gave her a chance to do something about clothes. Of course if she had been seeing him while she was still pretending to be Sally she could not have competed. Sally was rich. She would be expected to have fur coats and all those sort of things. But when she met him again just as herself she only needed to look smart in a not expensive way.

It's not easy to look smart on thirty-five shillings a week, even if you add a pound to that for tips and percentage. She gave her mother a pound a week. At the best she never had more than thirty shillings left for herself, often not as much. People had such different ideas about tips.

She gave a lot of anxious thought to the things she needed and the best places to get them. It was obvious Iris and Connie were the people to ask. They had masses of clothes. But there were drawbacks to going to them. First there was their terrifying suggestion of the friend of Iris's old man. Iris and Connie thought old men were made to provide wardrobes for working girls. Then, even supposing she could avoid that danger, there was Iris's and Connie's horrible interest to compete with. They would know at once why she wanted to be better dressed. It was this last thought that turned her against asking their help. Her feeling for Timothy and his perhaps for her had something elusive about it. Something as impossible to catch hold of as that unaccountable swell of gaiety that could sweep over you at the first sign of spring. Prying eyes, whispers and thoughts which saw love as a bargain window could spoil so ephemeral a thing.

She decided in the end on a little general advice. Roughly the girls were supposed to get from one till two for lunch.

Most of them did not go out. The gas stove Mr. Pert had provided was handy for warming things up. It was cosy, too, in the basement, a bit too cosy in the summer, for the boilers gave out a tremendous heat.

Ann was down to lunch early. She put the little cottage pie Alice had made her in the oven. She put on the kettle for everybody's tea. Kitty was already at the table eating. She looked up a little apologetically.

"Sorry, Ann. I might have done that. I've got a rush. Got a customer coming in at half-past." June, who was coming in, heard what she said.

"Who?"

"Mrs. Carlton. Never given anybody a tip yet."

Ann laughed.

"I wonder what the people who don't tip would feel like if they knew they'd a big black mark against them."

Kitty took a bite of the turnover she was eating. "Wouldn't care. That sort never does. I don't know why it is I get more of them than anyone else. Four of them! If they all come in the same week I reckon I'm down at the least five bob, and perhaps ten."

Biddy came bounding in. She had on her hat and coat, which were dripping.

"Gosh, it's wet."

"Well, why did you go out?" Kitty asked.

"I had an urge. I felt I must eat some crab." She held up a tin. "That and a couple of doughnuts."

"You'll ruin your figure," June said gloomily.

"Rot! What I say is a little of what you fancy does you good."

June sat sadly at the table.

"I wouldn't wonder if you were right. But I daren't risk it. I was at the League last night and I looked down the line.

There wasn't anybody bulged as badly as me. It shows up, too, in those black satin knicks."

Biddy cheerfully pried open her tin, looking with disgust at June's three slices of bread and butter and glass of milk.

"Thank goodness I'm thin. I'd just hate to eat that muck."

Norah came in with Agnes.

"Sure, and I'm hungry." She went to her locker and got out a little pie. She took it to the stove and put an arm round Ann. "Is there room for this?"

Agnes peered short-sightedly at the oven through her glasses.

"And mine?" She held out a rissole on some greaseproof paper.

Ann made room for everything. Norah hugged her ecstatically.

"And is she just a darling? You've the goodness of heart shining through you, my boyo."

Kitty looked up from her turnover.

"Iris and Connie have gone to lunch at some swell place in Jermyn Street."

"That's right." Biddy tipped her crab on to a plate. "It's with Iris's Perce and some boyfriend of his."

Ann pretended to be feeling how her cottage pie was going on. Really it was to hide the fact that she had flushed.

"Thank goodness," she thought. "Connie must have found time for him after all. That means they'll give up thinking of him for me."

"It beats me," Biddy went on, "how they can fancy those old men. I like somebody who can dance."

"So do I," agreed Kitty wistfully. "But we haven't all got rows of men to choose from like you have."

Biddy dug her elbow into her ribs.

"Snap out of it. We all know you wouldn't look at anyone else but Tom."

Agnes peered at Kitty over her glasses.

"When are you going to marry him?"

Kitty laid down her fork.

"Goodness knows. Sometimes I think it'll be never. You see, I can't fancy marrying him to live in the house with his mother. And he doesn't earn enough to keep up two places."

"Couldn't you go on working?" Ann suggested. "That would help."

"That's what I want to do, but Tom won't let me. He says when he marries he wants to keep his wife."

"Sure, then, I'd live with his mother," Norah burst out. "I wouldn't see all the best years of me life running away in loneliness."

Biddy choked over her crab.

"Hark at her!"

"If you knew Tom's mother," Kitty explained, "you'd understand. She's the sort that thinks no one has a right to her boy except herself. I'd mean all right to start with, but I'd be sure to have a row with her in the end."

June took a gloomy bite at her bread and butter.

"I haven't a boy. That's why I go to the League to get thinned down. They say there are a million surplus women. I get nervous sometimes I'm one."

There was a crash overhead. It was followed by hurrying feet. Then Lila's voice. They could not hear what was said, but there was no mistaking the tone.

"That's Betty." Ann took her cottage pie out of the stove and brought it to the table. "Poor kid. I wonder what she's smashed."

Norah looked round from the stove.

"Like as not it's everything on her tray. That Lila makes her fingers into thumbs."

Kitty sniffed.

"Old something! I'd like to wring her neck. She made the appointment for half-past one just to spite me. I heard her on the telephone talking to Mrs. Carlton's maid. 'Oh, no. Half-past one will suit perfectly. No, of course it's not inconvenient. The girl can have her lunch some other time.'"

"Makes me mad," said Biddy savagely, "to hear the way she talks to the customers about us. To hear her with a new one you'd think we were a lot of machines. 'Oh, yes, of course I can let you have a girl. Yes, quite competent. No, madam, we wind them up every morning. Mr. Pert would never allow their wheels to run down.'"

They were laughing when Betty came in. They stopped at sight of her. Her face was swollen and smudged with tears. Ann jumped up and ran to her.

"What is it?"

"It's her. Nosey P," Betty sniffed. "I'll have to leave. She makes me in such a state I just drop everything directly she looks at me."

"What did you drop this time?" Biddy asked sympathetically.

"All your containers of shampoo. I'd just mixed them. It's my day."

"Gosh!" said June. "What a mess."

"She's fined me half a crown for the stuff I've wasted," Betty moaned, "and I had meant to get a hat. I'm going to a cinema with a boy on Saturday. Now I'll be half a crown short."

Ann put her arm round her.

"Come on, don't cry. Where's your dinner? Is it in your locker?"

Betty nodded.

"Um. But it's only sandwiches—doesn't need to go in the stove."

Biddy stopped eating to pat her hand.

"Shut up crying and I'll give you a bit of crab."

"And if you want the hat this week," Agnes broke in, "I'll lend you half a crown."

Even all this kindness could not stop Betty's tears at once, but they did begin to subside. Ann felt she would recover better left to herself. Beside, the hat made a good introduction to her own clothes.

"Does anybody know a good place to go to get things that look good? You know, really good, but which aren't expensive."

Biddy stopped eating and opened her eyes.

"Dear! dear! dear! Who's the trousseau to dazzle?"

Ann managed to sound casual.

"Nobody, you idiot. Only I haven't a stitch, and the summer's coming. And I've got a bit in the post office."

Kitty got up. She went over to the glass and combed her hair.

"Would you mind second-hand if you knew they were all right?"

Ann looked doubtful.

"I'd thought of new."

Kitty powdered her nose.

"They mightn't fit, anyway. But I've a cousin works at Bertna's, the big dressmakers. She's in the showroom. They're allowed to buy the things after they've done with them. You know, after the mannequins have worn them. She's always said she'd buy things for me, but they never fit. I'm so big in the bust."

"She's tried to get them for me," Biddy joined in, "but I'm too small everywhere."

"It's a marvellous chance if you're the right size," Kitty explained. "They're lovely things."

Biddy nodded.

"You know. Slap up. Worn by duchesses."

Ann's eyes fit. It certainly did sound a chance. Those sort of clothes were just what Lady Mona and people of her sort wore. If she had hers from the right place, even if they weren't new, she would look all right to be seen out with Timothy.

"What do they cost?"

"Round about two pounds ten shillings, or maybe a whole outfit four pounds." Kitty crossed over to the washbasin. "All depends on the state they're in."

"How could I try them?"

Kitty spoke over the rush of water.

"Give me your measurements, and if you are right, I'll get some things along for you to see. Madame that runs the shop doesn't allow things sold outside except she knows who it is. She won't mind them going to you."

"Deed, and I hope they fit," said Norah.

Biddy swallowed the last of a doughnut.

"Don't wear them here, Ann, if they do. If you're dressed by Bertna's you'll make Iris and Connie look like twopence. They won't like that."

It was difficult for Ann to take her savings out of the post office and to buy a whole lot of new clothes without attracting attention from others besides Connie and Iris. There were, of course, her family as a start. Money being so short, anything new which came to the house was discussed down to the last thread. Even a little thing like a tie for Alfred, or a shirt for Bunny. Ann's new clothes had always come in for more discussion than anybody else's. On Saturdays and Sundays in the early spring and autumn mealtimes and so on were spent by Alice and Ann in earnest discussion as to whether the old blue would do one more winter or whether the silk would dye. When it came to new things Alfred and Bunny joined in.

"I wish you'd get brown, Ann," Alfred would say. "I like seeing you in brown."

"Oh, no, Dad," Bunny would expostulate. "Not brown; it's so dull. I wish you'd get bright red, Ann, or yellow."

The house interest didn't stop at her family; there were the boarders. It was not so much they said anything to Ann herself, but they discussed her appearance with Alice.

"I saw Miss Ann going out this morning. Makes you think spring's here to see her in that hat."

"My word, our Ann looked posh last night. Those plain frocks suit her style. Lucky I'm always in uniform. Wouldn't suit me."

"Very nice Ann looks in navy. Nice sensible things she wears. But I do wish girls wouldn't wear their hats at such extraordinary angles!"

"Oh, I say, Mrs. Lane, I do like Ann's new coat. It does suit her."

Ann, the gayest and most cheerful person in the house, had to be of universal interest. In a way she grasped this. She did not grasp just what she meant to them all. She just knew that they all cared what she wore. It was a nuisance now. She would far rather have gone round to Kitty's house and tried on the things. She would much rather when she had done her buying and got the clothes home have put them on casually one by one. These things she felt differently about to anything she had bought before. They were for Timothy. Only he could say if they suited her or not.

However, life was as it was; it was no good, she told herself, being selfish just because she felt sentimental. So one evening she came hurrying home from work and planted three dress-boxes tied together on the kitchen table. Alice looked at them in surprise.

"Have you won the Irish Sweep?"

Ann put her arms round her mother. She forced herself to sound more eager than she was. Alice mustn't guess that she had outgrown family conclaves.

"Second-hand, darling, but clean. Models from Bertna's."

Alice wiped her hands. Her eyes shone.

"Go on. Open them. What are they like?"

"I don't know. Kitty got them for me. She's got a cousin who works there."

Alice put her hand on Ann's.

"Now you give that to me. I can see your eyes looking up and down the dresser for my scissors. I don't want any good string cut here."

Ann watched her mother untie the knot.

"There's one is a frock coat and hat matching. There's one frock on its own. There's an evening dress and an evening coat."

Alice bent over the knot.

"Which were you wanting most?"

Ann's voice was carefully casual.

"Might get them all if they fit. It's a good chance. Mightn't come again."

Alice didn't answer that at once. Clothes never came to their house more than one at a time. Even second-hand, these would cost all the bit Ann had saved. Alice knew that Ann, the same as herself and Alfred, liked to have a bit she could fall back on. It was never mentioned, but it was accepted by them that with Bunny you never knew. As though Ann read her thoughts she said suddenly: "It'll take what I've got saved. If we need money for anything before I've put some more in I'll get a sub on my wages. Mr. Pert would, I know, if Minnie Briggs asked him for me."

"You've no reason to think of that." Alice's voice was gentle. "It's your money. There, that's undone." She stopped just as she was going to open the first of the boxes. "How about giving Dad and Bunny a call? They'll like to look."

"No!" The exclamation rang round the kitchen. Ann was horrified. It had slipped out without her will. "I mean," she explained, "I'd rather just you and me. They can see them when I've decided what I'll keep."

Alice's head moved up and her chin shot out as it did when she was going to argue. Then with quick control she changed her mind. She took the lid off the first box.

"Come on, then, let's have a look-see."

Ann was contrite. She hugged her mother.

"Oh, I am sorry. I am a beast. And Bunny does so love parcels. Wait a sec, I'll fetch them."

Alice looked after Ann. Her eyes were grave. What was all this about? Ann bringing home a lot of clothes didn't mean just nothing. They were for somebody. Somebody Ann, the most open of girls, wasn't saying anything about, wasn't bringing to the house. For almost the first time since she had borne her Alice was pricked by fear for her daughter. Of course, she'd been scared for her that time she had measles so badly, and that time she had the flu, which had left her weak all the winter, and that time she had that bad throat the doctor thought might be turning to diphtheria. But that was a different kind of being scared. She trusted Ann absolutely. She knew that if it came to a showdown Ann would be staunch to the way she had been brought up. But all girls could do silly things. Didn't she remember herself at that age, so ignorant and trusting, just wanting a good time? Ann was the same. Eighteen was always the same.

The clothes were beautiful. There was a navy blue frock, coat and hat, the frock trimmed with buttons made like lady-birds. There was a leaf-green evening dress. It had a little tight bodice held in with a great flaring bow. There was a tomato-red woolly frock which would go with the coat and hat of the navy outfit. There was a brocaded evening coat; it was almost military in cut, with squared shoulders and a little tailored collar, very tailored at the waist, where it went in to flare out to the floor.

"Put them on, Ann." Bunny hopped about in excitement. "Put them on."

"Now sit down, son." Alice laid a hand on Bunny's shoulder. "We'll make Ann put them on all right." She drew three kitchen chairs in a row. "We're smart people come to the dressmaker's to see what we're going to wear in the spring."

Alfred grinned.

"I do hope," he said, playing up to Alice, "that blue's in, my dear. I had hoped to wear that blue suit one more season."

Ann picked up the boxes. She laughed over the top of them.

"You wait. I'll give you a proper mannequin parade. Miss Ann Lane, England's foremost dress expert."

Ann wore the blue first because it was Bunny's choice. In fidgeting to see where it fastened she had it on before she had time to see the effect in the glass. When she did she stood still, her breath coming quickly. What a difference clothes made. This deceptively plain frock swept her away from the girl who went to work every morning. It took her just where she wanted to be, where she looked like Timothy's world.

The navy blue was so plain it deceived Alfred and Bunny and almost deceived Alice.

"It's nice," said Alfred. "I like the buttons." He walked round Ann thoughtfully. "But it's rather like you always wear. I thought coming from a grand shop it would be different."

Alice felt the material.

"It's good quality. I'd have that. It's sensible, and it'll stand by you."

Ann looked at her mother's face. Did she really think it was a good buy? Didn't she see how different it made her look?

It was the same with the tomato frock. They all liked it, but it didn't startle them. Didn't make them wonder who all this dressing-up was for. Gratefully Ann ran upstairs and put on the evening dress. For fun, because clothes as gay and useless seldom came into number 95 Anchor Street. Ann made an entrance in the green frock. She stopped outside the kitchen door, then flung it open, announcing, "The Lady Ann Lane."

"Gosh!" said Bunny.

Alfred felt suddenly against this dressing-up. Here was he, not even a chemist now. If Ann got around looking like that she would move away from their world. Alfred had put up with a lot. Only he knew what it had meant when his father died and his doctoring came to an end. He had known what was happening to his business long before he had told Alice. He had suffered, watching its slow strangulation, on his own. He had thought the day Bunny was born that nothing much would matter any more. He had a son who should do all the things he had missed doing. He had been a good athlete; he would have been a better if he had not had to work so hard, if his father had given him more encouragement to play. Nothing like that should happen to Bunny. He'd go to the grammar school and get into the teams. Life would be easier for Bunny; he would be willing to work with him at night. If his father had done that it would have been a wonderful help; it might have meant doctoring as a career. It had been hard the day the doctor had told them about Bunny's heart. Not that he hadn't known. He remembered enough doctoring for that. But hearing it in words the last hope died. It was then Alfred turned to Ann. In a life where nothing went right she was something to bless heaven for. So violently alive, so gay, so undaunted. He needed Ann about; she kept his courage and his faith going. He couldn't lose her to a world where he could not follow. It was that fear made his voice hoarse as he cried out at sight of the green dress:

"Take that off, Ann. It's pretty enough, but it's not for our sort."

Ann had spun round to show the bow at the back. She spun again at Alfred's words. She came across to him. She put her hands on his shoulders.

"Don't you say that to me, you old dreary. What sort am I? I'm Ann Lane, the grand-daughter of two doctors and the daughter of the best chemist that ever lived, and I'm as good as anybody in the country."

Alfred had a lump in his throat.

"Of course you are. Only you can't help mixing with people according to the money you have. There's nobody we know could take you to places where you'd need clothes like that."

Alice saw Ann's face. It was resentful. It was as if she wanted to say "If you don't know those sort of people, I do." She spoke quickly.

"Need! Hark at him, Ann. As if a woman ever chose clothes because she needed them. If we don't know anybody to take Ann to the right places for that frock, then the places she does go to must try and live up to Ann. How's that?"

Ann smiled gratefully at her mother, but she was not placated. She picked up the evening coat and turned to the door.

"I'll change," she said quietly. "We certainly don't need this sort of frock in our kitchen at supper-time."

On the stairs she met Miss Dean.

"Good evening, dear." She peered at Ann. "Have I seen that before?"

"No," said Ann.

"I do hope you won't think it interfering, but ought you to buy those sort of frocks? I mean they aren't very practical for a girl in your position. As a school teacher—"

Ann gathered up the skirts of her frock. She did not exactly push, but Miss Dean was edged on to the banisters as she shot past.

"Most unpractical," she agreed. "Thank you so much for telling me."

In her bedroom she pulled off the frock. She hung it up in her cupboard. Then she leant her face against it.

"Never mind what they say," she whispered. "I'll wear you, and you'll make me happy."

CHAPTER SEVEN

CORA was furious. She had been in that state since the wedding. In her own utterly selfish way she loved Timothy. Since she could toddle he had been part of her life. Long before she was supposed to be old enough to take in what was being said she was getting a kick out of the jokes of the grown-ups about herself and him. She had played up and looked wide-eyed, but inside she felt swollen and happy. They might laugh, but Timothy, who was so good at every-thing and so good looking that quite grown-up women liked talking to him, was hers, and always would be.

Even when he went up to Oxford and changed, she had thought it a passing mood. She had not been able to believe it that first term when he came down and forgot to ring her up. She was sure he had just taken it for granted they were riding as usual. To teach him a lesson she had started early and ridden alone. She had come back to find he had neither come round nor rung up. She had tried to get him back then. When she met him she had let him see she was hurt. He minded that, but not in the way she intended. He had been like a nervous horse veering away at sight of his saddle. He had broken out in a kind of fury, "Oh, for heaven's sake, Cora, haven't we outgrown that rubbish?" Even at that age Cora had been clever. Not by the flick of an eyelash did she show how much she was hurt, but quick as lightning she had flung up her head. "Silly old idiot, aren't you? I was only pulling your leg. Do you think I want you telephoning all day and all night?"

That had made things easier for a bit. At least he had felt easy with her again. She learnt her lesson quickly; she must outdo him in being offhand; that way he felt free. But clever as she was, Cora could not always override her heart. There were days when her whole body throbbed with the need of some affection from him. When she needed his arms round her so desperately she was incapable of pretending that she did not care a damn when she saw him again. When she had to try and excite him into making love.

She was always sorry for those occasions. It made him more casual than ever. He seemed to be able to flirt with half the women of London, but not with her. Somehow the memory of her at those early hunts, jogging behind him on her fat little pony, keeping him from jumping because in her blind faith in him she would jump too, had remained a violent memory. There were only two roles in which he could imagine her in connection with himself, sister or wife. She had always been the first. It's difficult to jump the mental chasm that can turn a sister into a lover. Cora knew that so far he couldn't or wouldn't jump.

There were, however, hopeful signs. There was at least nobody else; and he went about with her more than anybody. But since the wedding he had changed. Cora was fundamentally honest. She never had seen much point in kidding yourself about things. Now she faced the fact that the trouble was Sally.

The difference in him it took her lover's eye to discern. When you love a person yourself it's not all that difficult to see the same symptoms in someone else. She knew he was moody, restless, and sleeping badly. In a way she was almost glad of it. Why shouldn't he know how it felt for a change?

She was a bit surprised when he came and asked her if she had seen Sally, only surprised he had not done it before. General inquiries round her circle proved he was asking everybody the same question, and as nobody knew he was left where he started.

Then she dined with him on a Saturday night. Directly he called for her she felt a stab of fright. As the evening went on the fright grew. He was vague, he was illusive, he hardly ate a thing, but he was happy. "Blast!" thought Cora. "They've met."

Nothing that Cora had so far come up against could explain to her the game that Sally appeared to be playing. It had been obvious that there was some mystery about her. Cora had not forgotten that she appeared to be unable to speak French, that somebody who was known to be a bit of a tough drank scarcely anything and smoked nothing, that she shut up like a clam at the mere mention of South Africa and finally vanished into the night. Nor had she forgotten Iris. Nothing Sally said had blinded Cora to the fact that she knew Iris. Iris was certainly a queer friend for a friend of Mona's to possess. Besides, headache or no headache, it was odd the way Sally had vanished that night at the Savoy. But allowing for all these peculiarities, one thing was certain—she was a friend of Mona's, and any friend of Mona's would make a suitable friend for Timothy. Then why this disappearing act?

Unwilling though she was to admit it, Cora would have sworn Sally had been taken with Timothy that night at the Savoy. Then why?

Unable to bear not knowing for certain, she said at last:

"By the way, run into Sally yet?"

Timothy paused before he answered. Then his voice was as disinterested as hers.

"Yes."

Cora longed to say "Solved the mystery?" but Timothy's eyes had a restless look. She knew he would resent further questions and hold them against her. With great self-control she switched over the conversation.

Cora had a wretched night. Since that first vacation from Oxford she had faced Timothy's sisterly attitude. But facing it while she knew there was no other woman was one thing. Facing it while there was another, and what was worse, a woman he was meeting secretly was quite different.

"Blast her! Blast her!" she moaned. "She spoiled our evening at Mona's wedding, and now she's appeared again. I could strangle her."

She fell into a shallow unsatisfactory sleep at about five and awoke feeling terrible at twelve. She rang the bell furiously and cursed her maid for not calling her. She swallowed a little coffee, telephoned to put off a lunch engagement, had a bath, then, still feeling ghastly, mixed herself a large cocktail. The cocktail made her feel better. It lifted the tiredness for the moment, and it shifted the depression. She poured out another, then a third. Then she rang the bell.

"Tell them to bring round my car," she ordered her maid.

The maid looked at the cocktail-shaker. She often said in the servants' hall that Cora would kill herself one of these days driving when she was tight. On Cora's worse days she added, "And a good job too." But she never really felt like that. Now she screwed up her courage.

"Don't you think you ought to have a little lunch first? You've nothing in you but some coffee and—"

"All right, pussyfoot," Cora interrupted. "No need to be refined. Say a tumbler of gin and I'm tight. I don't care. I don't care about anything except that you order that car."

Cora drove out of London. She careered up the Watford bypass. She opened the sunshine roof and the air blowing round her head, mixed with the gin fumes, gave her a feeling of being on top of the world. She sang as she drove. She felt triumphant. What did Sally matter? What did anyone matter? She'd show them. A lorry had broken down. The traffic was jammed.

"Blast" sang Cora. "Blast the traffic! But it shan't stop me."

Without slowing she swung the car down a turning. The lane was narrow. She was going too fast. Suddenly there was a crash.

The crash startled Cora so much that it sobered her. With a completely clear brain she saw that she had knocked into a stationary car. That the other car was carelessly parked. That fortunately she had more grazed the other car than hit it, and no irreparable damage was done. And most important of all, in the other car were a man and girl who had been making pretty considerable love to each other. So considerable in fact that they still looked a bit dazed, and not because of the accident. Cora was quick to seize on an advantage. She got out of her car.

"What the hell!" she said. "Look at your damned car parked all across the road."

"I like that—" the young man began, hurriedly straightening his tie.

The girl laid a hand on his knee.

"No, George. Leave this to me." She turned with a charming smile to Cora. "I've got to throw myself on your mercy. I don't know who is to blame, but I'll pay."

"But—" Cora broke in, clinging to her advantage.

"You see," the girl explained, "my father said he'd take away my car if I had another accident. I've been ill; this is my first day out again. I'm taking it with me to the South of France tomorrow. You see how tiresome it'll be if I have a fuss with the police."

Cora turned and examined her car.

"It's just my mudguard, and this scratch on the door. Can I have the name of your insurance people?"

The girl opened her bag.

"Not my insurance because then my father'll know." She got out a card and a pen. "I'll put my solicitor's name. I'll tell them to pay up whatever it costs you." She passed over the card.

Cora took the card casually. Then she started. It said, "Miss Sally Groot," and gave an address in South Africa.

"I say—you aren't Sally Groot?"

"Yes. Why?"

"You were supposed to be a bridesmaid at Mona's wedding."

"That's right. But I started an appendix attack the night before."

"Then who was it instead of you?"

The girl passed Cora her cigarette case.

"God knows. Lady Manton turned up about two days after the wedding and said something about not letting anybody know it wasn't me. But at that time I was so swollen up with gas inside after my operation I didn't care who had done what, and would have promised anything."

"Didn't you know she wore your frock and said she was you?"

"No. As long as Mona's wedding went off all right I didn't care. In fact, it was a good thing. Father and Mother had gone back to South Africa, and they never knew I didn't make it, and they enjoyed no end swanking about it when they got home."

"Can't you remember a bit who Lady Manton said they'd got instead of you?"

Sally shook her head.

"Not a hope, old dear. I felt so ghastly while she was paying her call, it was all I could do not to cry. I never heard a word she said."

Cora flicked the ash off her cigarette. She gave Sally an all-girls-together look.

"I'd give a lot to know who it was. I've a reason."

"I wish as I've mucked up your car I could help, but I can't. But I tell you where I'm sure you could find out, and that's the Castle. Mona's maid, who held my head all night, has probably gone with Mona. But there's a cadaverous butler over whom I was sick while they were getting me on to a stretcher. He must know I wasn't at the wedding and who took my place."

"Hall!" Cora grasped the soundness of the advice. She turned back to her own car. "Well, goodbye. I shan't bother your solicitors. Not much harm done, and I'd just had a couple. It might have been my fault. Enjoy France."

Sally grinned.

"You bet. Good hunting to you."

Cora was never one to let the grass grow. That night she was on the telephone to the Castle and a day later she arrived there to spend the night. Since her meeting with Sally Groot she had made her plans. She discarded the Marchioness without two thoughts. That old diehard would never give anything way. The great thing was to keep her from knowing that she had anything to find out. Manners was away. That left Hall the only hope. Through the years Cora had known Hall. She knew his type. How he would sum up the guests by the amounts of their tips. Shouldn't be difficult to get news from him if you backed your questions with a fiver.

She did not catch Hall alone until the next morning. He was crossing the passage after answering the telephone. Cora beckoned from the empty morning-room.

"Hall, come here a moment." She closed the door. It was no good beating about the bush with Hall. No good pretending she wanted her information from laudable motives. Hall had everybody taped.

"I want to know who it was took Miss Groot's place at the wedding."

Hall's eyes shifted nervously.

"I never heard the name of the young person, miss."

"Young person!" Cora's heart beat quickly. Hall had very different ways of describing people. No friend of the house, not even an acquaintance, was a young person. She opened her bag and took out the fiver. She flicked it invitingly.

"Come on. This if you tell me."

Hall looked at the door to be certain it was shut. Then he leant forward and whispered.

Cora invited herself to dinner with Timothy. Before she had asked herself she had the evening clear-cut in her mind. She would find out if Timothy knew what she knew. If he didn't she would tell him. Playing about with South African heiresses was one thing, playing about with a girl from the Maison Pertinax quite another.

She waited till they got to the coffee and liqueurs. She took a sip of her Kümmel.

"Seen anything more of Sally?"

His eyes hardened.

"Why are you so curious?"

"Only I was wondering if she'd told you her real name."

"Her real name!" There was no mistaking the surprise in his voice.

"What are you talking about?"

Cora lit a cigarette. So he didn't know. Glory be! Well, now he should hear.

"Sally Groot was ill. Snatched off with an appendix. The bridesmaids' dresses being harlequin, they couldn't muck up the procession. Lady M looked everywhere and finally landed on the only possible—a girl from the Maison Pertinax hired to do Mona's face."

"What's her name?"

"Ann Lane."

"Ann," he said. Then he repeated it softly, "Ann."

"Fancy her not telling you," said Cora lightly. "She wasn't still getting away with being Sally Groot, was she?"

Timothy suddenly focussed her.

"I wonder why you've told me this."

Cora shrugged her shoulders.

"Old times' sake. Don't want you making an idiot of yourself."

"Idiot!" He smiled and said half to himself, "Poor kid. She did so want to explain."

Cora had a sudden horrid feeling he was taking her news all wrong.

"Well, I've saved her the trouble," she said harshly.

He lit a cigarette. Then he patted her hand.

"And done me one of the best turns you've ever done me."

"What do you mean by that?"

He grinned at her.

"You'll see. At least I hope so."

*

Timothy wrote to Ann. The letter was lying on Lila's desk when Ann arrived in the morning.

"Good morning," said Lila. "A letter has come for you. Mr. Pert doesn't like you girls having your letters sent here."

Ann glanced at the envelope. Who on earth, she wondered, would write to her here? Then she had a sudden thought. It might be Lady Mona. Perhaps she was home. She stretched out her hand.

"Sorry. I'll tell whoever it is not to write again."

Lila kept her fingers on the envelope.

"I'm not sure I oughtn't to show it to Mr. Pert."

Ann was fidgeting with impatience to see what was in the letter, but she knew Lila's methods. She shrugged her shoulders and moved off.

"Oh, very well. If you think he'd be interested."

The rule about letters was one of Lila's own. She doubted if Mr. Pert cared if the girls were written to or not. It was a rule which she had often found useful, for girls who were expecting letters usually made a bit of a fuss of her. They hung about and then blurted out, "If a letter came would she be a dear and let them have it at once?" Lila would purse her lips and say things such as "You know the rules." But she let it be understood that if they behaved themselves she might. All day, while they were waiting for the post, she felt their eyes on her and enjoyed her power.

But Ann wouldn't play. She never played Lila's game. Lila was convinced that rather than ask favours of her she would have let her burn the letter. With an ungracious jerk she pushed it to the edge of the desk.

"All right, take it. But don't let it happen again."

The other girls were downstairs changing. Ann went into a corner. She opened the envelope. At the address "Hill Street" her heart stood still.

My dear Sally Ann,

I have discovered your ghastly secret. You are a little fool, aren't you. Mona and Lady M might not want the news about the bridesmaid swap broadcast, as there'd be such a row with Aunt Lisa and her plain daughters. But that is not to say she would mind my knowing. I can keep a secret as prettily as any man in the land.

Since the awful truth is out, how about a bite tonight? I could pick you up at Maison Pertinax or meet you, anywhere you say. Give me a ring if you can manage it.

Yours,

Timothy.

PS.—Phone me at Victoria 51980; it's the Munster offices. Ask for Sir Timothy. Whatever you do, don't get put through to Sir Henry. He's my uncle. Head of the firm. Completely inhuman. Likely to give me the sack if he knew a girl rang me up!

Ann put the letter in her bag. Of course she was going to dinner with him. Her heart sang at the bare thought. But how it was all to be worked she had no idea. First there was the telephone. If you were very in with Lila you might be allowed to use it. But it meant a lot of fuss, and a lot of soft soap, and Ann certainly wasn't going to start that. Besides, the telephone was on Lila's desk, and apart from the fact that she could hear every word, so would all the other girls. Well, she knew the deadly hush which came over them during shop-dressing when one of them was on the 'phone. Every ear flapping for a bit of gossip. Then her clothes. Somehow she must get her new things from home. She was wearing just what she had been wearing when he met her on the Embankment. That wouldn't do. This time he had got to be pleased, and he had got to be proud. He knew now who she was, and he didn't care, and he had got to go on not caring; she must look so like the women of his world that he forgot she didn't belong.

Iris and Connie were her hope. Their lives were spent rocketing out of one difficulty to skid round another. Ann caught them before they went upstairs.

"I say, I've got to go out and telephone. Can you think of an excuse?"

Iris and Connie's eyes gleamed.

"Him?"

Ann nodded.

"But you won't say anything, will you? He's found out who I am, and he doesn't mind a bit."

"Sir Timothy Munster!" said Iris. "What a pity it isn't me or Connie. I wouldn't trust you to get a bit of imitation jade out of him."

Ann flushed.

"I don't want anything out of him. We're friends."

"Oh, yeah!" Connie winked at Iris. "Well, don't forget the song, 'When you grow too old to dream.'"

"You see, dear," Iris explained earnestly, "us girls simply must get a bit put by. It's our duty."

Ann knew that she and Iris and Connie could never think alike. She held Iris by the sleeve.

"How about the telephone?"

Iris looked at Connie.

"Lila doesn't like her," said Connie. She turned to Ann. "You should play up to her more. You never know when you'll need something. I don't know where us girls would be if we didn't play up to her for we're always back late after lunch."

Iris looked thoughtful.

"She'll have to need something at the chemists."

"But what?" Connie giggled.

Iris held up an admonitory finger.

"Keep the party clean." Suddenly her face lighted. "A finger stall. She's cut her finger."

"But I haven't," Ann protested.

"You soon will have. Look in my bag, Connie. I've some nail scissors."

"Ann. Iris. Connie." Lila's voice shrilled down the stairs. "What are you doing? It's seven minutes past."

"Sorry," Iris called. "Ann's cut her finger. We're washing it."

"Well, that doesn't take three of you."

"No," Iris agreed. "Go on, Connie." She held out her hand for the scissors. "You go up. I shan't be a second."

"Can't I help?" Connie whispered.

Iris shook her head.

"No. Go on up, you fool. Sorry, Miss Grey. But she's making an awful mess. I must just tie her up." She opened the scissors and made a scratch on Ann's thumb. "She's bleeding all over the place."

"Is she?" Connie whispered.

Iris bent over the scratch from which a few drops were beginning to well.

"She will. Hop it."

Ann, feeling a frightful hypocrite, went to Lila with her handkerchief round her thumb.

"Might I just go round to the chemist for a finger stall. I shan't be a minute."

Lila was suspicious.

"Let me look." Iris had done her job well. The scratch was bleeding nicely. Lila sniffed with annoyance. "Very well. But don't be long."

Ann was lucky to find an assistant at the chemists disengaged. She was not two minutes before she came out in a thumb stall. She ran to the post office, and dialled.

From the click as the dial connected, through the burr, burr of the bell, through the refined voice of the telephone girl who said, "Sir Timothy? I'll put you through to his secretary," through the crisp voiced secretary's "Miss Lane? Oh, yes, he was expecting you to call, hold on please," Ann's heart thumped. She was going to speak to him, going to hear his voice. Then suddenly it reached her.

"Is that you Sally-Ann? Aren't you the world's prize idiot?"

Her heart stopped thumping. It was as though she had been running through a tangled wood and suddenly she was out the other side and the sun was shining.

"Oh," she gasped. "I'm so glad you know. I've hated pretending to be somebody grand when I wasn't."

"Any more of that 'grand' talk," he said severely, "and I'll come round to the Maison Pertinax and put you to soak in Munster's soap flakes. Now, how about tonight? Suppose I fetch you at Pertinax at six or whatever hour you get out."

"Will you have your motorcar?"

"Yes."

"Then could you fetch me from 95 Anchor Street. It's off the King's Road. It's where I live."

"Must you go home first?"

"Yes. I'm dressed all wrong."

Timothy laughed.

"I bet you aren't. But can't I fetch you and drive you home and wait while you change?"

Ann considered that.

"No. I'd rather not. I mean I'd rather be all dressed when you saw me."

"Right. I'll pick you up at seven then."

"Oh, thank you. I must go. I'm not supposed to be telephoning. Goodbye."

CHAPTER EIGHT

ALICE was in her kitchen when Ann got in. For once she felt almost shy of her mother.

"I say, Mum, I'm going out."

Alice looked round with a pleased smile.

"Who with? Oswald?"

"No." Ann ran her finger up and down the table. "It's somebody I met at that wedding."

Alice didn't need to think. She saw it all suddenly. Ann's being so moody, and then the new clothes. Still, none of that mattered now. Ann wasn't keeping things secret any more. She wiped her hands on her apron.

"How about me coming up and helping you on with the new things. Is it evening dress?"

"No. He wanted to fetch me from the shop. It's just dinner somewhere. He's coming for me at seven."

Alice looked at the clock on the dresser.

"We'll have to hurry then. You go on up. I'll just find Dad and tell him to look out for your friend. What's his name?"

"Timothy. Sir Timothy Munster." Ann laughed. "You'll never guess. He's the soap flakes."

"Never! What, Munster the dirt away?"

"That's right."

Alice turned down the gas ring under her stew.

"I must tell Dad. He'll enjoy the laugh. I don't know how many times he hasn't said to me, 'You feeling Munsterish?'"

Alfred was more startled than amused by Alice's news.

"Munster! Must be no end rich. What's he want with Ann?"

Alice squeezed his arm.

"That's what you're going to find out. Behind your counter in your shop you were quicker at getting on to strangers than anybody I ever knew. See if you can get on to him."

Upstairs Alice showed no signs of her doubts as to Timothy's intentions. To Ann she seemed just as pleased about the evening as she was.

"I'm glad you've put on the tomato frock. Looks bright on a dull day. If you get time you might let Bunny see you."

Ann looked up from her cuff she was buttoning.

"Where is he?"

Alice's face clouded.

"I've put him to bed. He had one of his attacks this afternoon. Pain and was sick. I had to send for the doctor."

Ann sat down at her dressing table to put on her hat. Half the sparkle had left her. Alice patted her shoulder.

"Don't be upset. I wouldn't have told you only he'd be disappointed if you went out without seeing him."

Ann powdered her nose but her mind was on Bunny.

"What did the doctor say?"

"The usual. He says we ought to try and get him stronger in himself. He's so thin. He says he ought to be in the country. Asked me again about a home for children."

Ann looked up.

"What did you say?"

"I told him the truth. We'd let him go but he cries himself into an attack every time it's mentioned. The doctor was nice, said it was no wonder he didn't want to go away seeing the home he had."

Ann got up. She hugged Alice.

"So it is too. Hearing about Bunny makes me feel a beast I bought these clothes. If I hadn't you could have taken him to the sea for a week."

Alice laughed.

"And who would look after the boarders? You can't be in two places at once you know." She stood away from Ann. "I'm glad you bought them. You look lovely in them. Now you go and have a good time, and don't spoil your evening worrying about Bunny. What good's that going to do anybody?"

Bunny was sitting up in bed when Ann came in. He looked at her approvingly.

"Gosh, you look a swell. Where are you going?"

Ann sat on the end of the bed.

"Out. With a man I know."

"Who?"

"His name is Munster. He makes the soap flakes Mum uses."

"Can I see him? Will you bring him up?"

Ann did not want Timothy wandering over their house. Did not want him seeing the threadbare carpet, or running into the lodgers, but one look at Bunny's eager face and she buried her personal wishes.

"All right, darling. I'll go down and see if he's arrived."

Timothy was talking to Alfred and Alice.

"How do you do," he said cheerfully. "It's awfully nice of you to trust Ann to me. At least I hope you are going to?"

"Please come in and wait, Sir Timothy." Alice held open the sitting-room door.

"Thank you." He turned to her. "I hear you are a supporter of the family—Ann told me you always washed in us so to speak."

Alice sat down.

"That's right. It's good stuff."

"You use first class ingredients, don't you," Alfred put in. "I analysed it once. It's what I always say. You can't have a good product made of second-rate stuff."

"My Uncle George, who is a menace in the ordinary way, does keep the standard up. I'll say that for the old boy."

Alice twinkled at him.

"Don't you get on with your uncle?"

"You bet I do. He's my bread and butter. Awful old autocrat. He could turn me out tomorrow."

"Is it his business?"

"Yes, he started it. We were in shipping, then Uncle George dug up a recipe of a great-grandmother. It was written in an exercise book. It was headed 'Recipe for washing linen whyte.'"

Alice was interested.

"My word, it would surprise your great-grandmother if she could know the money it made."

"A good thing it has. It's all there is to keep the wolf off the old doorstep. When my father died he left me nothing but the baronetcy and you can't eat that."

Ann came in. It made her shy seeing Timothy with her family. She felt suddenly all hands.

"Oh, I say," she said abruptly, "I've a little brother, he's called Bunny. He's ill. He wants you to say good-night to him."

Alice's mind raced. She, too, thought of the threadbare carpet, and she remembered that Bunny had on his old dressing-gown with the piece on the elbow that didn't match, and that it was Thursday and the sheets had been on the bed since Monday. No, she didn't want anybody as rich as Sir Timothy going up just now. It would be a different thing if she knew he was going and had prepared for him.

"Sir Timothy won't want to stop now," she said hurriedly. "I'll explain to Bunny."

Ann looked across at her mother. Her eyes said, "I know it's a pity he's got to see it but it's what Bunny wants so he's going to."

Timothy had got up.

"Poor kid. What's the matter with him? Of course we'll go and see him."

"He's got a bad heart," Alfred explained. "Congenital."

"I'm afraid his room won't be very tidy," Alice apologised.

Timothy laughed.

"I was in bed once for three weeks, you should have seen mine."

Bunny was shy when Timothy came in. But Timothy was not going to let him get away with that. Half the frieze of bird transfers was up and that made a good opening topic. Timothy did not know much about transfers but any amount about birds.

"Interestin' little fellows," he said. "I'll send you along some books about them. No good having an owl over your bed and not knowing how the old boy lives."

There was no quicker way to the Lanes' heart. Timothy was embarrassed by the exclamations of pleasure from them all. Bunny, overcome, said:

"Gosh. Do you mean for my own?"

Timothy nodded.

Alfred cleared his throat.

"It's very kind of you. Very kind indeed. He hasn't many books."

Alice's eyes shone.

"Well, that will be something to look forward to, won't it, Bunny?"

Ann said nothing but her face spoke volumes.

They left after that. In the car Timothy was silent for a bit.

"I'm sorry," said Ann timidly, "to have bothered you to come up to Bunny. But he was so pleased."

"Bothered!" Timothy's voice was rough. "Made me feel such a cad the kid and all of you being so pleased about a few books."

"Well, it was nice of you," Ann said simply. "You see we haven't much money for those sort of things."

He took his hand off the steering wheel and patted her knee.

"I daresay between us we can think of a lot of things he'd like."

They went to The Ivy. All restaurants were alike to Ann, who knew none. Timothy said they would in the course of time do all the good ones. Then she must decide which she liked best and they'd make that their headquarters. After going to the same place about twice the Maitre d'Hotels would know her by sight and welcome her, and going to that particular place would be like going home.

Ann let all this chat about how the rich lived blow over her. It might be true. If Timothy said so it probably was. Certainly everyone had known him at The Savoy. But it wouldn't happen to her and she didn't care. All she wanted was to sit near him and for him to go on talking.

That dinner was a revelation to Ann. She had never thought of famous people eating anywhere, certainly nowhere where people like herself could see them. But that night they were surrounded by them.

"That's Marie Tempest," said Timothy. He looked at the menu. "I could eat a dozen oysters. How about you?"

Ann had never eaten oysters and never seen Marie Tempest except on the stage. Marie Tempest won. "Is it really her?"

Timothy laughed.

"All right, I'll deal with the food. This is a very literary and theatrical place. In the corner there is Dodie Smith. By the door is John Gielgud. And that's Jessie Matthews and Sonnie Hale."

Ann felt dizzy. Such a plethora of fame.

"And they all look nice," she said. "I mean people one could talk to."

Timothy finished ordering the dinner. Then he leaned forward and looked at Ann.

"Of course they are. But what I want to talk about is us."

There is never greater fun than when a man and a woman knowing each other to be attracted start to probe each other's depths. To Timothy and Ann it was as though they were deep-sea divers. They slipped through the water of the everyday world and were cut off by themselves. And down there they made discoveries. Twists in each other's characters. Twists of mind. Tastes they had in common. Tastes totally different. Across that table they began to learn each other and were deaf and blind to what they were eating and who was round them.

"Tell me about being a beauty specialist," said Timothy, "is it fun?"

Ann screwed up her face in thought.

"It isn't bad. It isn't exactly what I'd have chosen but it's all right."

"What would you have chosen?"

Ann sipped her wine.

"Funny how things seem to matter desperately at the time and then you outgrow them and they don't matter any more. We weren't always as hard-up as we are now and Dad had a savings account for me, it was a joke and he called it 'Ann Investments, Ltd.'"

"Very nice too, ought to be well supported."

She laughed.

"Aren't you silly. There was a bit put to it every month. It was to train me for whatever I wanted to do."

"And what did you want to do?"

"It sounds awfully serious. Best of all I'd have liked to be a doctor but there was never enough money for that, and my second choice was a chemist. I had a scholarship at the Fall Secondary and it's awfully good on that sort of thing. I wanted to be an analytical chemist. Awfully grand ideas I had, hadn't I?"

He nodded.

"Matter of fact I must admit my tastes have run the other way. You know silly, brainless little women."

She shook her head.

"I don't believe that."

"Well, what stopped you going all analytical?"

"Money. First Dad's business went down, and then flats went up and they put in their own chemists on the premises. That finished him. Then Bunny was so ill, illness simply eats money. Dad and Mum tried not to, but they had to dip a bit into 'Ann Investments, Ltd.'"

"Poor Sally-Ann. Did your family know about your ambitions?"

"No, wasn't it lucky, I'd never told them. I don't know how it is with boys but girls get awfully reticent round about fifteen. Then of course when I saw the money going I deliberately kept it from them, after all, no good everybody being in a gloom."

Timothy passed Ann a cigarette which she refused.

"And you chose to be a beauty specialist?"

Ann leant forward, her chin on her hands, her eyes sparkled with amusement.

"That's an awfully rich thing to say, most girls, and boys too, I daresay, never chose the job they're in. They just happen."

"How did you land on your particular brand then?"

"I was leaving school. Dad wouldn't let me go into untrained work, he said it was a dead end. It was urgent I should earn money quickly so I chose the face business. There was nearly a hundred pounds left of 'Ann Investments, Ltd.' A place called 'The Wolstone School of Beauty Culture' offers to train you for fifty pounds and guarantees you a job. Inside I was so sick at not being able to be a chemist I didn't care what I did, so here I am."

His face was concerned.

"I call that a rather miserable story. It must be a beast of a job, messing about with the faces of lots of women who've more money than sense."

Up shot Ann's chin.

"Don't you believe it. Your job is what you make it. I've stopped having even a lingering feeling about chemists. I love my work."

"You can't."

"That's all you know. You think it's all fiddling about with make-up, but it isn't."

"But don't they chatter like a lot of magpies at you?"

"Sometimes, but I don't really listen. You know, your fingers get very sensitive. No matter how much they're talking what I'm really thinking is, 'Here's a muscle sagging. I wonder if I can tighten it,' and I'm hoping the customer will come in regularly so that I can make a good job of what I've started."

He looked at her appreciatively.

"I think Maison Pertinax are lucky to get you. What are the other girls like?"

"Nice. All sorts you know. Minnie Briggs who does faces with me is an angel."

"Don't you ever have rows?"

"Not with Minnie Briggs. I've only had one with the girls." She smiled reminiscently. "It was after I'd been there a week," she raised her eyes to his. "Looking back I think I must have seemed an awful prig, but I couldn't help it. Everybody's got their own ideas of what's right and wrong."

"Tell me about it."

"In hairdressing shops the rule is the customer is given a check and they pay it at the desk as they go out. At the end of the week the girls get commission on all their customers. One and eight in the pound. Well, sometimes the customer's in a hurry and says, 'don't bother with the check, how much is it?' And the girl may say ten and sixpence or whatever they owe, and when the customer's gone makes out a check for perhaps eight and sixpence."

"And pockets the difference."

"Yes, it sounds awful, but it's done sometimes by girls who think they can get away with it."

"Sounds a silly sum to cheat over."

Ann laughed.

"That's because you were born with a silver spoon in your mouth, but if you're us, two shillings is a lot."

"But you don't do it?"

"No. I think it's cheating. The time I was talking about, a girl called Nancy was caught at it and sacked. Well, downstairs when we were having lunch they were all saying what a shame it was to sack her and of course I said nothing. Then one of them said to me didn't I think the punishment was too hard. And I said 'no,' it was cheating and if you cheat you can't expect a firm to keep you. They were furious but I had to say it. You can't help what you think."

He saw the young new Ann in the shop dining-room standing up to all her fellow workers and he had a sudden longing to squeeze her hand. He resisted the temptation and made his voice light and easy.

"No. But we haven't all got the guts to say what we think."

"Oh well." Ann laughed. "They've got over it now. I knew they would in the end." She lay back in her chair. "I've been talking an awful lot about me. Tell me about you. Did you want to sell Munster soap flakes?"

Timothy tapped his ash thoughtfully on to the tray. "Yes, I think I did. We're shipping people as I was telling your mother, and ships are like women, they get under your skin, but it's no good crying for the moon."

"We're alike in that."

"Yes. Only I haven't learnt to get fond of my job because it is my job, after ships it was my second choice." Ann unconsciously raised her eyebrows.

"Really! You don't look a bit the sort of person who would have anything to do with soap."

"You wouldn't know about that. Proper little soap king he is." He paused. "Would the story of the Munster soap flakes bore you?"

"No. I'd love to hear it."

"Uncle George's great-grandmother lived to the ripe old age of ninety. She was born in 1694, Harriot, spelt with an 'o,' Boles, her name was, and she married a man called Shrew. Shrew was a clever fellow. He grew up in the reign of Queen Anne, you know, 'dead as Queen Anne,' and she, poor creature, had a bit of trouble with her children."

"More than trouble, they all died."

"That's right. Clever girl knows her history book. Well, it was evidently an unhealthy date or something, anyway dying children were fashionable and old Shrew made a wonderful herb garden and set up as a kind of Great Ormond Street. Legend has it in the family that Queen Anne sent for him about one of her children. But I suspect that's family snobbery and not based on fact. However, there's no question he was a very smart fellow."

"Did the great grandmother look after the children too?"

"No. Queen Anne was dead before she married Shrew and sick children out of fashion, but Shrew made a nice living as a travelling quack who went round the fairs and so on, and my uncle's great-grandmother Harriot stayed at home and minded her children and the herb garden, and that's where the Munster soap flakes come in. Amongst the herbs was one with a very sweet smell. In that date, as you know, women wore a lot of lace and stuff falling out of their sleeves and tucked in the front of their frocks and petticoats. Well

Harriot, on Monday in Holy Week, so she says in her diary, was washing her finery for Easter Day, and stepping out to hang something on her line she was struck by the smell of one of the herbs in the garden. 'That will make the other girls in church sit up,' she thought, and picked some of the flowers and threw a handful in with the smalls. Apparently a miracle happened, the water did whatever the best water does on washing days and the clothes on the fine were, to quote the old lady, 'whyte as maybloom with a sweetness as of honey.'"

"What is the herb?"

"Ah! Our secret, Madame. Uncle George being struck down with influenza happened in boredom to turn up Harriot's diaries, spotted the bit about the herb and the answer is Munster's flakes."

"Is that true?"

"Yes, absolutely. As a matter of fact I'm rather proud of it. I think it's fun. I like to think people like your mother are getting the same kick Harriot got two hundred years ago."

Cora came into The Ivy at nine o'clock. She was dressed to go to a reception. She looked even more lovely than usual. Most of the diners looked up, but two people never moved. Cora, seeing she had not attracted their notice, glanced at them. As she walked across to her table the man with her saw her pause and where she was looking.

"Old Timothy," he remarked. "Shall we go over and give him a chyak?"

"No." Cora smiled at the headwaiter. "Give us a table in the corner somewhere."

Her partner took up the menu.

"Oysters?"

She composed her face.

"I don't care a damn what I eat. But I want the hell of a lot to drink, and make it snappy."

*

Cora came in at three o'clock. She was tight. Her maid heard her come in. She pulled on her dressing gown and her slippers and ran to her room. One look at Cora told her experienced eye how she was. She quietly began to undo her frock.

Cora looked round.

"Lousy evening."

"I'm so sorry, Miss. If you'd just stand still a minute I'll get your frock off."

Cora put her hand on the dressing table.

"How the hell d'you expec' someone who's as drunk as I am to stan' still."

The maid laughed nervously.

"I'm sure you're not, Miss. Now, if you sit I'll take off your shoes and stockings."

"Course I'm tight. So would anybody be who had to put up with what I've had to put up with. It's a terrible thin' to trus' a friend and be let down."

"Yes, Miss."

Cora was too confused to remember exactly how she had been hurt but she was carried away by self-pity. She began to cry.

"Let down by bes' friend."

"It's a cruel world, Miss. Now come on and sit on your bed and I'll put on your nightie. You'll be asleep in no time."

The maid was right. Cora was asleep in about ten minutes. She woke at eleven with a bad hangover. Her mouth tasted like the bottom of a parrot's cage looks. She felt vaguely sick. Her head throbbed. Feebly she rang the bell.

"Some of my mixture and a glass of bromoseltzer.'"

The maid was used to Cora. She ministered quickly and sympathetically.

"I'll bring black coffee in half an hour," she said, and went out.

By the time her mixtures were beginning to do their work and she was sipping her coffee, Cora saw the morning. The sky was tinted with the first touches of blue. Spring was in the air. It looked as though it would be nice in the country. It would be nice to hunt. A thought struck her. How would it be if she could get Timothy to come down for the weekend? It would give her a chance to talk to him. He must be crazy to go hanging about after a little shop girl. She had thought letting him know who she was would be bound to finish it. It wasn't even as though she was a chorus girl; they had something. But a girl in a hair and face place! It was an impossible sort of friendship. If only she could get him to herself and did it tactfully surely she could laugh him out of it.

She picked up the telephone and dialled.

Timothy's voice came cheerfully over the wire.

"Hullo, duckie. How's things?"

"Fair to lousy. I think I need a bit of exercise. How would it be if you came down for the weekend and we had a hunt?"

Timothy laughed.

"No such luck. I daren't make it. Uncle George has had me on the carpet about my weekends. He says when he was a boy his working week was Monday morning until Saturday night and 'We were the better for it, by jove, yes.'"

"Blast him." Cora settled herself more comfortably against her pillows. "Well, come down on Saturday afternoon. We'll get in a hack on Sunday."

There was the shade of a pause before he answered.

"Sorry, my sweet. No can do."

Had Timothy seen her he would have caught the most vicious look in Cora's eyes. "It's that little snake in the grass," she thought. "He's going out with her." However she managed to make her voice silvery.

"What a shame. Got a date?"

"That's right. Well, I must get back to my soap flakes. I'll give you a tinkle sometime and we might eat a chop one night. So long."

Cora put down the telephone. Her eyes were thoughtful. There had been no mistaking the tone in which he had said, "That's right." It meant, "Yes I have and it's my secret so hands off." A secret date could only mean one person. Always before he had said, "Sorry, I'm footing it with Primrose." Or "I'm taking Diana to a show."

It was a damned nuisance about Saturday. He was always nice out hunting. Still, it was probably true about his Uncle George. Awful old autocrat. Very Victorian ideas.

She sat upright. Very Victorian ideas! That gave her an idea and not a Victorian one either. Suppose Uncle George heard about Ann Lane? He would soon make the devil's own row. Pretty shop girls would not be at all his idea of companions for his nephew.

She hugged her knees feeling enormously better. Telling Uncle George was undoubtedly the best idea she had landed on in weeks. The only question was how to tell him.

CHAPTER NINE

Timothy arrived at 95 Anchor Street after lunch on Saturday. He had his arms filled with parcels.

"These are for Bunny," he said to Alice. "Can I go up?"

"He's down on the sofa. My word, he'll have another attack when he sees these."

Alfred, Ann and Alice all stood round watching Bunny's face while he opened the parcels.

"A book on birds. A storybook. A book of birds to paint and a paint box."

"And I've left a box of chocolates behind," said Timothy.

Alfred shook his head.

"He's got more than enough. You're spoiling him." But his face was pleased. With the little money they had Bunny seldom had new things.

Timothy looked at Bunny.

"He's made the wrong answer. You were meant to say 'Why did you leave the chocolates behind?' Go on."

"Why did you leave the chocolates behind?" Bunny asked obediently.

"On purpose because I want to bring them tomorrow."

"So you can see Ann?"

Timothy nodded.

"Got it in one. I never was a person who could keep a secret. I expect you think wanting to see girls is a waste of time."

"Seems a bit sissy," Bunny agreed.

Timothy grinned at Ann.

"Your brother scorns my low tastes. Come on. I'm not going to offend his eyes by making him witness my blind devotion. We're going to the sea."

"Now?" asked Alice. "Going to the sea's an all day job, you can't start now."

Timothy laughed.

"It needn't be. My car can fairly nip along."

Alfred shook his head.

"I daresay you'll think us old-fashioned, but we're not used to fast cars. They make us nervous."

"Really!" Timothy found that extraordinary. "Well, I tell you what, I'll have Ann back here by seven-thirty. Cross my heart and hope to die."

Alice smiled.

"Young men have made those sort of promises before."

Timothy looked at Bunny.

"You hear that? She's insulting our sex. You'd trust me, wouldn't you?"

Bunny raised a radiant face from behind his bird book. "Of course I would."

Alfred gave a grunt.

"After all those presents he'd say anything."

"But honestly I'll have her back at seven-thirty. I'd hate you to be worried."

Ann slipped her arm through her father's.

"You won't worry will you, Dad? It's such a lovely day, and if he says half-past seven he means it."

Alfred looked at Alice. His face said: "I don't like it. All this dashing about the country in motorcars with rich baronets, and you read of such awful accidents."

Alice returned his glance, her eyes said: "I know, old dear, just how you feel, but we mustn't be spoilsports must we?"

Alfred squeezed Ann's hand against his arm.

"All right. Get along then. But not a minute after seven-thirty." He turned to Timothy. "She's precious to us you see."

"Where are we going?" asked Ann as they settled in the car.

He put his foot on the self-starter.

"Sussex. Somewhere I know that's nice and spacey. I hate a crowd."

Ann, in a trance of happiness in being with him, did not care where she went. The going was slow out of London but once clear they flew along.

"Oh, look," said Ann, "bluebells."

Timothy nodded.

"Myself I prefer my bluebells at Whipsnade. There's something about bluebells and wolves on the same afternoon that gives me a kick."

Ann's town eyes could not drag themselves from the fields and hedges. Spring had come suddenly, leaving a trail of flowers and green leaves and baby buds and animals in her wake. Even the staidest of the beasts felt her stirrings in his blood, not a carthorse but had an extra toss of the head. Not a bird but had a love song or chirp to give.

Timothy raised his head and sniffed.

"I smell the sea." He drew the car up, and nodded at a couple of thrushes. "With so much affection going round is there any reason why I wouldn't have a little?"

Ann flushed.

"Well—"

"Once I kissed your cheek. Do you remember?"

She smiled. Did she? Had she forgotten one thing he did, or said?

"She doesn't remember, faithless hussy, and a kiss in a vestry should be sacred. It has more or less the blessing of the church. Come on now. Timothy will do it again."

Other people besides themselves had fancied the sea, but at that moment theirs was the only car in the lane. He put his arm round her and with his other hand tilted her chin. There seemed a hush everywhere as their lips touched. Either they could not hear them or really for a moment there was a cessation of chirps, and of branches creaking in the wind. It was as if the birds looked down from their nests and held their breaths, then, as Timothy released Ann, they let themselves go, never was there such a to-do. "Did you see that, my dear?"

"Evidently human beings can do sensible things sometimes."

Timothy stared at Ann in a dazed way.

"You do seem the answer to dreams, don't you?"

She rubbed her cheek against his shoulder.

"I didn't know one could be so happy."

They were lucky, as Timothy drew the car up under a sand dune, before them stretched as far as eye could see, deserted beach. It was early in the year for sitting about but Timothy found a windblown hollow in the sand. He wrapped a rug round Ann.

"Now sit there quietly while Uncle Timothy fetches the tea basket."

Ann's eyes shone.

"A picnic. What fun. But don't we need sticks and things for a fire?"

Timothy looked scornful.

"These cave-women! No, darling, we don't, we use a stove."

It was an enchanted time. They said very little while they watched the kettle boil. That feeling of nearness, and your own personality flowering because of someone else's, was with them both. Any words seemed banal to express such happiness.

"There," said Timothy at last, "the kettle's boiling. I know it is because steam's coming out of the spout."

Ann gave him the look she usually kept for Bunny.

"Aren't you clever."

He opened a cake box.

"Cake, biscuits, or I can do a very nice line in sandwiches, Madam."

Their peace was broken by a man and a girl about their own ages. The young man was rolling up his trousers.

"Bit of luck if it fits," he said.

Timothy opened his eyes.

"Now I wonder what's going to fit what?"

"He's going to paddle," said Ann.

Interested, they watched the couple walk down to the sea. The girl had the man's shoes and socks. He got a grip on his trousers well above his knees and began to wade out.

"Look, it's a buoy or something," said Ann.

Timothy shook his head at her.

"The ignorance of the woman. That, my girl, is the inner tube of a tyre."

Seeing somebody wade out almost to the point of getting wet after something bobbing just out of reach, has the same entertainment value as watching a person run after a blown-away hat. Timothy and Ann sat enjoying the entertainment and liking the feeling of enjoying the same joke. An extra large wave carried the tyre a bit further out; the young man made a lurching grab after it and almost slipped; his girl, who was giving advice from the beach, gave a little scream.

"Be careful, Bob. No good getting drowned for it."

Timothy got up.

"Young idiot, I believe he can't swim and the tide's going out."

Ann and Timothy joined Bob's girl at the waves' edge.

"Can that young man of yours swim?" Timothy asked.

The girl shook her head.

"No."

Timothy raised his voice.

"I say, you'd better let that go. There's quite a strong tide, it's not worth drowning for a tyre."

Bob turned, grinning.

"That's all you know sir," he waded in. "Have you got a walking stick, I think I could just reach it then."

Timothy shook his head.

"Sorry. What do you want the tyre for?"

"Well, sir, you see, Rose's mother—this is Rose—doesn't care for her going out on my motorbike and she cuts up rough if we're back late, so Rose promised we'd be home by six for tea."

"And so we would have been," Rose put in, "but he's got a puncture."

"Well, can't I help with that?" Timothy suggested.

Bob looked sheepish.

"The outer tyre wasn't too good, getting very shaky, and I went over where somebody had broken a bottle, and cut the inner tube to bits; take a terrible time to mend if you could mend it."

Ann pointed at the floating tyre.

"Is that tyre for a motor bicycle?"

Bob nodded.

"Yes. Seems in nice condition, too, far as I can see."

Timothy turned to Ann.

"Would you take Miss Rose for a walk the other side of the sand dunes. This is where I show how I won third prize in the under thirteen swimming at school."

Ann and Rose walked up the beach.

"It's nice of your friend," said Rose. "It's such a way to push a bike to a garage from here and I don't suppose they could do much and Mother won't half be in a state if I'm late."

Ann looked sympathetic.

"Don't I know. My mother's made us promise to be back at half-past seven." They were by the car; she opened the door. "Shall we sit inside out of the wind?"

Rose looked in awe at the car.

"What a lovely car, Miss."

Ann laughed.

"Don't call me Miss. My name's Ann. Where have you got to get to?"

"Croydon." Rose stroked the leather of the seat: "I wouldn't half like to go out in something posh like this, course Bob's bike's all right but you do get a bit bumped."

"I suppose you do. I've never been on a motorbike and as a matter of fact hardly ever in a car."

Rose looked surprised.

"Haven't you? Well! I thought—I mean—"

Ann nodded.

"You mean you thought people like me always went about in them, but you see, I'm poor. I work in a beauty parlour. This car isn't mine."

There was a "Hi!" from behind them and Timothy and Bob came over the dunes proudly carrying the inner tube. Ann felt motherly. Timothy, with his hair on end from the water, and the proud strut that a child gets when it has been clever, was very endearing.

The tube did fit. In a few minutes Timothy and Bob had it in place.

"Can't thank you enough, sir," said Bob. "Piece of luck coming into a new inner tube like that."

Ann and Timothy went for a walk up the sands. They strolled arm in arm in a nice wordless companionship. The seabirds me'ewed. The wind twanged the grey-green sedges. The dusk came up softly like the dimming of a candle. Timothy squeezed Ann's hand under his arm.

"Nice knowing you."

At the bend they came on a policeman. He was standing by something lying on the sand.

"What d'you suppose he's got there?" asked Ann.

Timothy looked up idly.

"Perhaps it's a shark." As they drew nearer he caught at her arm. "Better turn back, my sweet. I'm afraid it's an accident."

Ann raised her chin.

"Turn back! Perhaps I can help."

They could see now what it was. On his back lay a young man, dressed in nothing but his pants. Timothy looked at the policeman.

"What's happened?"

The policeman sucked his pencil.

"Found drowned."

The man was half in the sea. Every wave splashed him and seemed to be trying to drag him back saying, "We killed him. This is our prey."

"Hadn't we better move him up the beach a bit?" Timothy suggested.

The policeman shook his head.

"No. Never touch a body washed in by the sea, not without you're wearing India-rubber gloves."

Timothy looked round.

"But will you find any india-rubber gloves here?"

The policeman's voice took on an official police court tone.

"On viewing the body, I dispatched Jo Smith, who found the deceased when digging for bait, and told him to telephone for same."

Timothy looked at the dead man.

"Well, let's hope the gloves come quickly, or he'll wash out to sea again."

"They'll bring 'em in a boat. Here any minute now." He opened his notebook. "How old would you say he was?"

"Twenty-two, twenty-three."

Ann felt a lump in her throat and turned away. After saying she would help it seemed weak-kneed to be caught crying. Still, it did seem miserable to be twenty-two or twenty-three and drown on a fine Saturday afternoon.

"Wonder how long he'd been in the water," mused the policeman.

"Take a doctor to say that."

"That's right."

"Wonder how it happened?" said Ann.

The policeman shook his head.

"No saying. Lot of people drown and no one knows how it happens."

The policeman made notes in his book. Timothy took hold of Ann's arm.

"Come on, let's go."

She shook her head.

"No. It's bad enough to be drowned all by yourself, but it's worse to be carried off by the police all by yourself. It's like having nobody to go to your funeral. I think he'd be glad if we stopped."

The three of them stood in silence. It was getting cold; they watched the waves suck the dead man a little further down the sand. Suddenly there was a distant chug-chug and a motorboat ploughed its way towards them.

Another policeman and a man got out of the boat. The gloves were produced and solemnly pulled on.

"Not room for him on your boat is there?" the first policeman asked the man.

The boat owner shook his head.

"Got a bit of board for him."

The body was strapped on the board and covered with a piece of tarpaulin. The board was then fixed to the stern of the boat, and the two policemen and the boat owner got in and they chugged out of sight with the tarpaulin-covered thing bobbing behind them.

Timothy and Ann turned away. Ann shivered. Timothy looked at her anxiously.

"Are you cold?"

She shook her head.

"It was a goose on my grave. That—" she nodded at the distant tarpaulin shape, "made me think. Being happy is awfully important, any time, even tomorrow you might lose your chance of being."

They walked on in silence, climbing up the beach to the sand dunes. Over the top of one in a hollow they came on a motor bicycle. It was propped against a bank of sand. Tools lay round it, the back tyre was off, in a heap by the tools lay the owner's clothes, a quick glance at the tyre showed them the inner tube was missing.

"Must have taken it for a swim to use as a lifebelt," said Timothy.

Suddenly Ann was crying. He took her in his arms.

"Don't cry, sweet. They say drowning's one of the better sort of ends."

"It's not that," Ann choked, "but it seems so mean. There's Rose and Bob gone back on his tyre to get home in time for tea and there's him—the tyre came as a miracle to Rose and Bob, why couldn't he have had a miracle, too? I suppose a wave washed it away from him. Why couldn't another have washed it back again?"

He drew her on and they got to the car. He put her in, then felt in one of the pockets and got out a flask. He poured a little brandy into its cup.

"Drink that."

Obediently she swallowed it down. He got in beside her and pushed the self-starter.

They had gone quite a way before he spoke again. It was in the lane where they had kissed. He put his arm round her.

"I was wondering whether if that young man knew all he'd done he would grudge either you and me, or Rose and Bob, what he'd given us."

"Given you and me?"

"Yes. I felt as we stood looking at him as if I'd got a squint at something I'd always missed. You gave it, and he gave it. I'm a fool at saying what I mean, but between you I got on to something that really matters."

"What?"

He kissed her gently.

"I'll tell you some day but not now."

*

Sir George Munster was a man of habits. He believed in regular hours. He had a house at Weybridge. So regularly you could set a clock by him he came out of his front door at nine o'clock every morning. With just three minutes in hand he caught the nine-seventeen to town. Every evening he was on the platform at Waterloo at five twenty-five and caught the five twenty-nine home. Every Saturday he caught the twelve-sixteen. There was not an employee at the Munster offices, nor a porter at Waterloo that did not know his habits.

On Saturday morning a porter flung open the door of a first class carriage.

"Good morning, Sir George. Beautiful day."

"Splendid." Sir George got in and sat in his usual corner. "Hope you young fellows get out in the air a bit this week-end. Nothing like it. Only way to get an A1 nation. Though mind you mustn't let the open air interfere with Church."

The porter was having the afternoon off and was snatching the chance to work at his allotment so he answered rather pompously:

"Yes, indeed, Sir. I'm having a day tying up my young peas." He hesitated, struggling with his conscience, for he was a truthful man. "So I shall tomorrow, after church, Sir."

Sir George snorted with pleasure. This young man was after his heart. Not much wrong with Britain when his sort were about. He felt in his pocket and got out a shilling.

"Nice old buffer he is," the porter said to a friend. "He's Munster's soap flakes. The missus swears by 'em."

"Wouldn't mind having a bit of what he makes by 'em."

The porter tossed the shilling on his palm.

"I have, and all for opening a carriage door."

His friend nudged him.

"There's a lady getting in with him. He won't like that."

The porter shrugged his shoulders philosophically.

"Neither he will, poor old geezer. Still, can't do nothing. Trains off."

Cora sat down in the corner facing Sir George. Luck was with her. The carriage was empty. So much easier to do your stuff in an empty carriage.

Sir George, after one infuriated glance at her, settled down behind his *Times*. What did women want jumpin' into first class smokin' carriages. He didn't wonder the country was goin' to the dogs. With the women goin' to pieces what could you expect.

"Isn't it Sir George Munster?" said Cora sweetly. "I expect you've forgotten me. I'm Cora Bolt."

Sir George put down his paper. Cora Bolt. Lord Brixton's girl. Stupid of him to forget. Hadn't seen her since she was a child. She was the one everybody thought young Timothy was marryin'. And a suitable match too. He hated to talk in the train. Still, if she was Cora Bolt he supposed he'd have to. Time young Timothy settled down.

"Why of course, my dear. You're a friend of Timothy's."

Cora surreptitiously took the glass stopper out of a bottle of smelling salts. They were so powerful they made the hardest eye fill with tears.

"We were," she agreed in a well-rehearsed tone of tragedy.

Sir George examined her. "Nice little thing," he thought. "Plainly dressed. None of that nasty paint on her nails."

Cora, looking wistfully out of the window, saw Sir George's face in the glass. She felt pleased with herself. It was clever of her to have dressed the part and though it made her feel a hag it was particularly clever to have taken the enamel off her nails. No woman could really please an old man while her nails were painted.

"We don't see so much of each other now, of course," she added.

Sir George looked at her sharply.

"Why not? Boy been annoyin' you?"

"No." Under cover of her handkerchief Cora moved the salts bottle nearer to her nose. She was rewarded by feeling her eyes flood. "I thought you knew."

"Knew what?"

Cora raised her eyes and two tears rolled down her cheeks.

"I'm a fool to go on caring. I never thought he was that sort of man."

Sir George was always moved by a woman's tears. He leaned over and patted her hand.

"Now then. What are you talkin' about? What's my nephew been doing?"

"Well—" Cora took another secret sniff at the salts. Her tears flowed faster. "He hadn't said anything but it was understood we liked each other."

Sir George patted more fervently.

"That's right. That's what I was told."

"Then somehow he met a girl."

"Girl! What girl?"

"Oh, nobody you know. Just a little hairdresser's assistant or something."

Sir George snorted. Hairdresser's assistant! In his young day it had been the chorus. But whoever they were they didn't mean much. Just a wild oat or two and then settle down. Of course a nice girl like this Miss Bolt wouldn't understand that sort of thing.

"I don't suppose it means much, my dear."

Cora gave a very good imitation of a sob.

"If only it was like that I wouldn't mind. But I'm afraid he's fond of her."

Sir George stopped his patting. His eyebrows bristled.

"Don't mean he might be such a fool as to think of marrying her?"

Cora nodded, tears streaming down her cheeks.

"That's what I'm afraid of."

Sir George's face took on the look it wore at a difficult board meeting.

"What's her name?"

"Ann Lane."

"Umm." He got out of his seat and sat next to Cora. He took one of her hands in both of his. "Dry your eyes, my dear. I may be an old man but there's life in me yet. Quite enough to bring young Timothy to heel. Now you stop frettin'. In another week or two shouldn't wonder if you could announce your engagement."

Cora, under pretence of mopping her eyes, withdrew her hand and managed to slip the smelling salt bottle on to the seat and sit on it.

"Really?" She looked at him ecstatically. "Could you do something? I mean without ever telling him I told you? He wouldn't forgive me if he knew it was me."

He gave a harsh chuckle.

"I can, my dear."

At Weybridge Cora watched Sir George disappear up the platform. Then she put her feet on the opposite seat. She lit a cigarette, and smiled happily at the carriage roof.

Alfred and Alice did not know what to make of Timothy. For all Alfred's sharp summing up of people, a gift of his which had increased with his shop experience, he couldn't place him.

"I do feel," he said anxiously to Alice, "I ought to ask him what he's after. He won't see it, but Ann's terribly fond of him."

Alice smiled.

"Must be blind then. The boarders say he's just as fond of her as she is of him."

Alfred frowned.

"I don't like everybody talking over her affairs."

Alice laughed. She was cooking. Expertly she cracked an egg on the edge of a basin. She paused while she separated the white from the yolk.

"If you know a way to stop boarders chattering you're a clever man. Besides half of it's niceness. They look on themselves as the family."

Alfred walked to the window and beat a tattoo on the pane.

"I don't know what to make of him. He doesn't act as I did when I was after you."

Alice looked up from her stirring. Her eyes twinkled. "How do you know how they act when we aren't there to see? Kissing's not gone out of fashion from all I hear."

"Well, he's always so offhand. You know, laughing and teasing her. He said to her last night, 'Come on, you old hag, you.' That doesn't sound as if he were fond. I mean, not in love."

Alice laughed.

"You aren't moving with the times. Besides, what he says in front of us and Bunny's one thing. What he says to her when they're alone is another." She put down her wooden spoon and bowl of mixture. She joined Alfred at the window. She rested her hand on his shoulder and her cheek on her hand. "I wouldn't say anything to him if I were you," she suggested gently. "If it's all right and he's fond of her there's no need. If it's all wrong and he's just playing her up you won't do any good either. She's so happy she won't thank you for ending things."

"If he goes now without saying anything he'll hurt her."

"Course he will." Alice's eyes were soft. "But we women are funny you know. If we're fond of somebody we'll go about with them, however much it hurts, and like it."

*

Sir George looked at Timothy over his glasses.

"Come in, my boy. Shut the door."

"If it's about those sale figures at Birmingham," said Timothy, "I can explain—"

Sir George held up his hand.

"It's not. Just want a straight talk. I hear you're about with a little shop girl—" Timothy took a step forward. Sir George stopped him. "One minute. I'm not blamin' you. But I would like your assurance it's nothin' serious." Timothy's face was white.

"Well, you won't get it. It is serious. The only thing I've ever been serious about in my life. I want to marry her." Sir George turned plum coloured.

"What's that! You know what you're sayin'? My nephew marryin' a girl like that. I won't have it." Timothy's eyes glinted.

"I don't know who's been gossiping to you but aren't you taking too much on hearsay. Ann isn't the sort of person you describe as 'a little shop girl.' And, my word, when you see her you'll apologise."

"No I shan't because I'm not seein' her." Sir George paused. "Nor, if you go on with this foolishness, will I be seein' you either."

Timothy stared at him.

"You can't mean—"

Sir George nodded.

"Don't get excited, my boy. But have a look how things are. I made this business. Worked it up from nothin'. Thanks to it you're pretty well off, and I'm a rich man. Now riches are a responsibility. Get into the moneyed class in this country and certain things are expected of you. Marryin' little shop girls isn't one of them."

Timothy held himself back from hitting his uncle. "Don't keep calling Ann that. It's an insult to her and to all shop assistants in the country. Do you think because a girl has to earn her living it makes her less respectable than the rich?"

"Well, maybe not. But you know how it is. Havin' to make ends meet makes them a bit casual how they do it."

"God!" Timothy turned away. "You make me sick. How do you think half Debrett come by the clothes they wear?"

Sir George cleared his throat.

"We're not discussin' the morals of society. We're discussin' our own family. What I'm tellin' you is that it's a case of the girl or your job."

Timothy came to the desk. He leaned on it and glared at his uncle.

"You puffed up old snob. You think money is so important that you have the idiocy to believe a man would give up a chance of marrying the girl he loves because of it. Well, you can keep your dirty job. Goodbye."

Timothy was taking Ann to a first night. It was the first outing for the green frock and its accompany-coat. Alice waited to hear Ann leave the bathroom, then she came up to help with the dressing.

"They all want to see you dressed," she said as she knelt and fastened the tiny hooks that ran under the great flaring bow.

Ann fingered the folds of her frock.

"I hope he'll like it."

"Fancy a first night!" Alice sat on her haunches and looked up at her daughter. "I don't know what there is about the sound of one but it makes you think it'll be exciting."

"Would you like to be going, Mum?"

"You bet." Alice got up and took the evening coat off its hanger. "When you were little Dad and I often went to the theatre. It was usually Saturday night. We used to go early and get places in the pit. I often used to look at the stalls, which is where you'll be sitting, I expect, and think it must be nice to sit in them. You know, no standing, no rushing, just drive up to the entrance nicely dressed. That would be all right I used to think."

Ann put on her coat.

"Poor Mum. It's a shame you've never had anything."

"What!" Alice gave her a quick hug. "Silly girl. I've had everything. A good husband. Nice home, and both of you. I wouldn't change places with anybody. Not even Queen Elizabeth!"

Ann laughed.

"I can see you at Buckingham Palace. Before you'd been in the place two minutes you'd be down in the kitchen interfering with the cooking. Then upstairs interfering with the Princesses' lessons."

"I certainly would," Alice agreed. "Why, I make a row about four boarders about the place. How'd I get on with Ladies and Gentlemen in waiting under my feet all day?" Maggie Dean popped out of her room as Ann went by. "May I just look, dear? Sweetly pretty. Though myself I always like white on a young girl."

Oswald Perkins leaned over the banisters. He whistled through his teeth.

"Hullo. Is that Greta Garbo. I can't see very well from here."

Mr. Bloom was waiting in the passage outside the sitting-room door. He tried to pretend that he was not there on purpose.

"Good evening, Miss Ann. If I may say so you look charming. Perfectly charming."

He sounded like somebody who had not seen anything nice for a long time. Ann took off her coat. "Do you like the frock?"

Mr. Bloom seemed quite silenced by what he saw. At last he said:

"Oh, yes indeed. Oh, indeed yes." Then he turned to Alice. "One forgets, you know, in a dusty office from nine till six."

"Forgets what?" Ann whispered to her mother when they were out of earshot.

"That there are still some nice things in the world. Come on, silly."

Alice made quite a show of presenting Ann to Bunny and Alfred.

"What d'you think," she said. "Cleaning out the bath I found a fairy had got caught in the chain of the plug. I didn't like to throw her away so here she is. She'll give you each a wish."

"Gosh, Ann. Don't you look nice," said Bunny. "I wish you could give wishes."

Alfred felt once more upset by Ann in her finery. It made him remember his suit was shiny and green with age. It made him wonder if she couldn't travel so far from them that she would be lost.

"But she can give wishes. And don't go calling her Ann. She's Fairy Loofah. That's why I found her in the bath. And I'm having the first wish." Alice thought a second. She gave a nod at Bunny. "May as well make it a good one. If you please, fairy, I'd like a motorcar."

"If she's granting that," said Alfred, "let's hope she gives the money to keep it up."

"Please, fairy." Bunny's voice was excited. "Could I have a house in the country with a garden."

"Don't want much, any of you, do you?" Alfred observed.

"Come on, Dad." Ann tucked her arm into his. "What do you want?"

Alfred squeezed her hand.

"Something you really can grant. I don't want you going so far away that we can't get at you."

"Why should I?" Ann looked puzzled.

"There's other ways of going away than travelling," said Alfred.

Ann didn't follow him. Alice saw her confused face. "Don't listen to him, the old silly. Hark, there's the bell. That'll be Sir Timothy."

CHAPTER TEN

"WE WON'T have dinner," said Timothy. "There isn't time. We'll pop along to the Berkeley Buttery for a snack, and then we'll have something at the Savoy Grill afterwards."

"Two new ones," said Ann. "I am getting on with my education in restaurants."

Timothy, to her surprise, did not answer at once. Her training in West End restaurants was one of those jokes two people who are fond of each other always share. Not funny really, but easy to laugh at because it's between you.

"Have you acquired a taste for rich eating, Sally-Ann?"

Ann looked up.

"Of course. Why shouldn't I? I've got to like oysters and smoked salmon and Mont Blanc made of marrons and lots of things."

He glanced down at her.

"Got to like them so much you'd miss them?"

Ann noticed his tone was serious, so though she thought food did not matter much she thought about it seriously.

"I should think the more you do things that cost money the more you'd miss them."

"So you," said Timothy gently, "only having moved in rich ways for a few weeks wouldn't miss them much?"

"No," Ann agreed.

He cheered up after that. He made her laugh so over some smoked salmon sandwiches at the Buttery he made her choke. At the theatre he pulled her into a corner of the foyer.

"Come here, duckie, and watch the publicity hunters do their stuff. See that fair woman. That's Lady Gloria Wish. She pays God knows what to some publicity fellow to keep her in the news."

"What for?"

Timothy shook his head.

"The dear knows. Now watch."

Ann watched. A rather got-up looking man touched one of the cameramen. The fair woman was standing apparently talking to a man friend but in reality watching all the cameramen out of the corner of her eye.

"That rather caddish-looking fellow will be her agent merchant. He's on the carpet tomorrow if she isn't photographed."

There was a blinding flash. Lady Gloria went on talking to her man friend as if she did not know what was happening.

Timothy laughed.

"There's one publicity agent can go to bed happy tonight."

"Will it be in the paper?"

He nodded.

"*Tatler* or something."

"Goodness," said Ann. "Fancy being in a paper."

There was another flash. Timothy looked up.

"You'll soon know how it feels. That was us."

One of the camera assistants came over.

"Would the lady mind us giving her name, Sir Timothy?"

Ann had a sudden vision of the gossip at the shop if she was featured.

"Oh, please, no."

Timothy took her hand.

"If you don't mind, darling. It's one of the best things that could happen." He turned to the man. "This is Miss Ann Lane."

The play was one of the ever-popular family stories. Generations of family strewing the stage. The programme glittered with great names. The audience were enchanted. But Ann could only give half her mind to what was happening. What on earth had Timothy meant, "It's one of the best things that could happen."

"I think," said Timothy when they were at the table in the Savoy Grill, "I could do with a nice bit of haddock a la Maison. You fond of haddock?"

Ann had never considered haddock a thing you ate at that hour of night, but she was learning.

"I'd like some too, please."

Timothy ordered the drinks. Then he lit a cigarette.

"Would you mind marrying a poor man?"

She opened her eyes. What was he asking for? What did he know about poor men?

"Of course not. I wouldn't mind who I married if I was fond of him."

"Wouldn't you mind if he was out of work?"

"You mean on the dole?"

"Not quite, but nearly."

"Course not. Loving hasn't anything to do with things like that."

"Hasn't it?" He leaned forward and played with her fingers. "I wish I could believe you. I'm going north tomorrow. I want to see a friend in an aeroplane factory. I might work for him."

Ann gasped.

"Are you going to give up your soap flakes? I thought you liked being with your uncle."

"Uncle and I have had a few nasty words. I've left."

"Do you think you'll get a job on the aeroplanes?"

"Don't know. I'll be up there going through everything. If I seem intelligent I might."

"I shall miss you."

He stroked her fingers.

"When I come back I've something to ask you."

She flushed. The conversation had made it obvious what he would ask.

"I don't think you having a job matters."

"I know you don't, precious. But the boy has his pride. I can't go to your father and say, 'I want to marry Ann but I'm afraid all I've got is about enough to keep a dog.'"

"Your idea of what it needs to live on and ours wouldn't be the same. I mean we'd probably think enough to keep your sort of dog was being rich."

He gripped her hand.

"You're the nicest person in the world. I'll be back on Friday. Will you dine, and in that frock? Please. Because then perhaps I can say my piece properly."

Ann's eyes were unexpectedly misted with tears.

"Friday," she whispered.

The picture was published the next morning. Cora saw it during her breakfast. She choked into her coffee.

"The fool," she thought. "Doesn't he care a damn what happens to him?"

She looked at the clock. It was after ten. That old idiot Sir George would probably be at his office. Those sort of old bores always get up early, called it setting a good example or something. She picked up the telephone and dialled.

"Is that you, Sir George?" she asked sweetly. "It's Cora Bolt. Have you seen *Daily Pictures* this morning?"

"What's that? *Daily Pictures*? Never see it. Vulgar."

"Only there's a picture in it of Timothy and her. They were at the first night last night."

Sir George made an odd sound down the phone. It was as if he were tearing a length of calico in half. Cora took the receiver from her ear and waited for the noise to subside. When she listened again he was saying:

"That settles it. I told him to go and I mean it." There was a pause and his voice could be heard roaring, "Miss Jones. Miss Jones. Send out for a *Daily Pictures*. Get it at once." He returned to Cora. "Silly young ass. Well, let him try marrying without a job. See how he likes that."

Cora's heart gave a sudden jump, so violent it hurt. So Timothy did mean to marry the girl. It had only been a guess in the dark when she had said it to Sir George.

"Does he know just what it means?"

"Ought to. I told him clearly enough it was the girl or the job."

Cora said a polite goodbye. She put down the receiver slowly. Her face was white. Suddenly it puckered. She turned over and buried her face in the pillow. So it was going to happen. All she had hoped for snatched away in a minute. All finished because of a bit of ill-luck that a bridesmaid had an appendicitis. It was the wildest fluke that had given Timothy a chance to meet Ann.

Exhausted with crying Cora lay on her back and stared at the roof. It's no easy job when from childhood you've pictured yourself with just one man, to rebuild without him. Cora tried but she simply could not do it. Could not see a future without Timothy.

"I can't bear it," she whispered. "I can't bear it."

After a time she roused herself. She picked up the telephone again and dialled Timothy's flat. His man was there. He was full of information.

"He's gone up north, Miss. He is seeing over the Pinstead aeroplane works."

"He's thinking of joining them, isn't he?"

"I believe so, Miss. He said this morning he couldn't seem to see himself living up north. But he supposed he'd get used to it."

Cora put down the telephone. Evidently it was perfectly true. And it was her fault in a way. If she hadn't said that to Sir George things might never have come to a head. She had been a jealous idiot. Likely as not Timothy was only marrying the little wretch because his uncle said he couldn't. He was like that. She would not even then have thought he would be mad enough to give up his place at Munsters. Not only his place now but what it meant in the future. After all, Sir George wouldn't live forever. The girl must be pretty caddish to take such a sacrifice.

Cora sat up.

"Take such a sacrifice!" Did Ann know? Perhaps he had never told her. Perhaps there was still a chance.

"Who?" said Lila. "Oh, yes, Madam."

"Now look!" Cora's voice was rapid, but very charming. "I want my face done by Ann Lane. But I wonder if you could be very kind and not tell her it's an appointment with me. It's just possible she might want to avoid me."

"Oh" Lila's eyes widened with excitement. "Of course. Yes, Madam."

She put the telephone on its stand and made an entry in the book. She went over to the beauty specialists' cubicles.

Ann was working but Minnie Briggs was disengaged.

"There's an appointment for Ann at two o'clock. See she is back sharp from lunch."

Minnie Briggs raised her eyebrows.

"If you saw anything further than that nose of yours, Lila Grey, you'd know Ann is never late for an appointment."

Lila bridled.

"Maybe not. But there are things. Mr. Pert isn't altogether satisfied."

"No?" Minnie Briggs got up. "Then I'll be along and see him and ask him what's wrong."

"You take me up so," said Lila. "I didn't say there was anything to complain of. It's just his manner."

Minnie looked disgusted.

"Oh, get along. You make me sick. Bully, bully, nag, is your motto."

Minnie Briggs caught Ann just before lunch. She spoke in a whisper.

"You've somebody coming in at two so slip on down to your lunch."

"I've got a customer now."

"Who?"

"A Mrs. Marion. Mud pack."

Minnie grinned.

"You watch me."

The customer with wool pads over her eyes, and a mud mask on her face, was lying on the couch. Minnie bent over her.

"I'm taking you now, Madam. I'm the senior skin specialist. Mr. Pert likes me to have a look now and again at every customer."

The customer made an appropriate sound of approval at Mr. Pert's thoughtfulness. Minnie winked at Ann and gave her head a jerk towards the basement.

Biddy looked up from a plate of tinned salmon.

"Hullo, here's the Queen of Sheba."

Ann went to her locker and got out her steak and kidney pie.

"Don't look much like it today. I've got on my old blue."

Biddy nodded.

"What's happened? He left you?"

Ann flushed.

"Don't be so silly."

"I wish you could get me a frock from Bertna's, Kitty," June said wistfully. "I'd like to look like Ann."

"It's not Bertna's, old dear." Biddy swallowed a mouthful of salmon. "It's the shape."

"I know. But it's not that I don't try. There's no one goes to the League more regularly than I do."

Agnes peered at Ann through her glasses.

"I don't know what it is but something's made you prettier lately, Ann."

Ann, scarlet in the face, turned round from the stove. "Aren't you an idiot."

Betty looked up from her sandwiches.

"I've always thought her pretty."

Norah took a spoonful of soup.

"And you'd be right, my boyo. It's the blessed light that's shining through her."

Biddy choked over her salmon.

"Ann won't get a hat on if you go on like this."

Kitty moved up to make room for Ann.

"You ready for any more clothes?"

Ann shook her head.

"I'd like some but I'm afraid to spend any more. My brother's not too good. You never know when you want a bit saved."

"That's the truth." Kitty poured herself out a cup of tea. "But even saving doesn't help when you want two houses. One for your mother-in-law and one for yourself."

"If I was your Tom," said Biddy, "I'd give the old girl an arsenic sandwich. Her sort are a nuisance."

Ann took her pie out of the stove.

"It seems dreadful, an old person spoiling everything for two young ones. I mean, when you are fond of a person it would be terrible not to be able to marry them."

Biddy took a cream bun out of a bag.

"'Ark at 'er!"

The door opened. Iris and Connie came in. Biddy paused with a piece of cream bun half way to her mouth. "Hullo. What's happened. The Ritz closed?"

Iris looked at Connie. Connie nodded. They came across to Ann. Iris, suddenly, like a conjuror producing a rabbit from a hat, held out a copy of *Daily Pictures*. It was folded so that the picture of Ann and Timothy was uppermost.

"I take it the cat's now out of the bag?"

"No. I mean, please don't say anything."

"*Daily Pictures* is a paper anybody might buy," said Iris. By this time the whole table had stopped eating.

Biddy swallowed a mouthful of cream bun.

"Do you mean Ann's picture is in *Daily Pictures*?" Agnes got up.

"Let's have a look."

June followed her.

"Come on, let's see."

"Oh, please, no," said Ann, trying to pull the paper from Iris.

Iris shook her off and turned round.

"Look at that. Miss Ann Lane and Sir Timothy Munster at last night's premiere."

"Gosh!"

"Look at her."

"That's the things I got her from Bertna's."

"Sure and she looks a darlin'."

"I wish you wouldn't breathe over my shoulder. You make my glasses cloudy."

"I can't help it. My stomach takes so much room I have to lean if I'm going to see. It's not my fault. I'm always at the League."

"And me and Connie knew all the time," said Iris.

Connie nodded.

"But us girls can keep a secret. But of course if she's going to have her face in all the papers everybody's got to know."

"He looks a lovely boy," said Kitty.

Iris nodded.

"He's marvellous. Going the places me and Connie go, we know him quite well by sight. When I saw Ann with him the first time, I said, 'My word, that's a bit of all right, all right.'"

June sat down again.

"How'd you meet him, Ann?"

Iris and Connie rushed to tell the story first. They had never had such an audience. They told it in bits. As soon as Iris paused for breath Connie broke in, and vice versa.

"Then not long ago," said Iris, "she had a letter."

"She simply had to telephone," Connie explained.

"So I cut her finger," Iris broke in. "She said she had to go to the chemist for a finger stall."

"And," Connie concluded triumphantly, "she's been going out with him ever since."

The girls were speechless for a moment. Then Biddy spoke for them all.

"Fancy it happening to you, Ann. You don't seem a bit that sort."

Ann, still crimson in the face, looked up.

"What sort?"

"Well, you know, the sort that sort of man takes up with. Now if it had been Iris or Connie, or even me—"

Iris sat on the end of the table.

"Pity it wasn't. I bet if it had been us girls we'd have made more of it. Being Ann, it's all lovely while it lasts and nothing to show for it afterwards."

"Sure and what do you know?" Norah's voice rose with indignation. "And mayn't he love her whoever she is?"

Iris giggled.

"Love!"

Kitty took a gulp of tea. She spoke to Norah with an almost motherly air.

"You mustn't get muddled in London. Men as rich as him don't marry our sort."

"But they can be very useful in their way," Iris added.

Ann threw up her head.

"Don't you believe them, Norah. They make everything sound so beastly." She turned to Kitty. "Timothy's not like that. He's nice, like your Tom. He's—"

"Ann." Lila's voice came down the stairs. "It's two o'clock. Please come up for your customer."

"And you've not eaten your pie," said Agnes.

Ann got up.

"I don't want anything."

Iris shook her head at Ann's retreating back.

"Poor little cow. She's got a nasty jolt coming."

Ann smoothed her couch ready for her customer with shaking fingers. How hateful it had been. What she was to Timothy and he to her was her own business. It would be nice if she could have silenced them all by explaining she was engaged to him. After all, she would be after Friday. She had not worried about his talk of no job and quarrels with his uncle. In her inmost heart she thought it would be nicer if he were poor. Poor people had each other so much more to themselves without servants always about. Besides, it would be fun saving and working to make his money go a long way. You couldn't do that if people were rich. They didn't care where the money went and you couldn't work for them, they would rather hire someone to do it.

But what the girls said hurt. She knew Timothy loved her but it smirched things somehow if everybody felt it was impossible. It was as if she were dragging him down if she married him.

"I'm not," she told herself, angrily sorting out her bottles and pots. "Love hasn't anything to do with whether you make soap flakes or massage peoples' faces."

"This way, Madam." Lila's voice came up the passage. Ann smoothed her coat and turned to greet her customer.

Cora stood a moment in the entrance.

"You!" said Ann.

"Good gracious. It's Ann Lane," said Cora. "Or should I say Sally Groot?"

Lila stood outside, her ears flapping.

"What was this? Sally Groot?"

The telephone bell rang. "Drat the thing," she muttered and went back to her desk.

Ann, in a daze, stretched Cora on the couch and mechanically began to work her face.

"How did you know that I was me? I mean, how did you find out I wasn't Sally Groot?"

"I met her. She told me. Lady Manton told her. Any case of course I'd know now. We've always known the Munsters."

Ann's fingers mechanically moved swabs soaked in cleansing lotion over Cora's face. Mechanically she threw the soiled swabs into a container. Mechanically she took lumps of cream on her fingers and began to massage. What did Cora mean? "Any case of course I'd know now." Timothy couldn't have said anything. He wouldn't before he had asked her.

"You're marrying him, aren't you?" said Cora.

Ann's heart thumped.

"I don't know. I mean, I think so. You see he's had to go up to the north."

Cora sighed.

"Awful for him. Tell me, does he mind dreadfully? I mean, it must be pretty devastating having everything you've worked for and come to expect swept away in a minute like that."

Ann's trained fingers did not stop moving.

"What are you talking about? Do you mean because he's left his uncle?"

"Yes." Cora lay silent a moment. "You must be a very brave person. You know, I wouldn't dare let a man smash up his life for me. I'd always be afraid that one day he'd hold it against me."

Ann found the muscles that ran under Cora's chin. Her subconscious mind said to her fingers, "There's a tendency to sag here. Give it a good tightening up." Her conscious mind was staggering as though it were giddy.

"What have I to do with his smashing his life?" Her voice did not come out properly. It was a whisper.

Cora sat up.

"Do you mean you don't know?"

Ann shook her head.

"No."

Cora patted the place beside her on the couch.

"Sit down." Ann sat. "He went to his uncle and he said he wanted to marry you. He explained, of course, who you were. His uncle said if he married you he must leave the business."

"Why? He's never seen me."

"He's ambitious for him."

"What did Timothy say?"

"He was awfully upset at first. Tried every way to get the old man round. Offered to put off being engaged for a bit, and said could he have time to think things over."

"Timothy did?"

"Don't blame him too much. Of course he's fond of you. Everybody knows that. But it takes the hell of a lot of being fond to be worth smashing your career. After all, he's used to having everything."

"But he did choose to smash it."

Cora hesitated. Then with great friendliness she took one of Ann's hands.

"No. As a matter of fact his Uncle George was so angry he wouldn't give him time to think. While he was balancing things up he was sacked."

"Oh!" Ann sat quite still, gazing at her hands. Then she gave herself a shake. "Hadn't I better finish your face?"

She only spoke once more during the massage.

"Do you think his uncle would take him back? I mean, if there wasn't me."

Cora could hardly resist a triumphant wriggle.

"Certain to," she agreed casually.

Her face done Cora looked in the glass.

"You're a very good masseuse." Ann said nothing but held out her coat. Cora put it on. Then she opened her purse and took out ten shillings. She passed it to Ann. "Thank you so much."

Ann looked at the note. Then she looked at Cora.

"You ought to know better than that. Good afternoon, Madam."

"Satisfactory massage, I hope," said Lila, hurrying after Cora to the door. Cora looked at the note in her hand and laughed.

"Very." She gave Lila the money. "Thank you so much."

CHAPTER ELEVEN

Ann had finished her day in a trance. She had learned that if you are sufficiently trained you can go on functioning without any help from your conscious self. As she massaged and put on mudpacks, and gave vibro-treatments, her mind raked over every word Timothy had said. All those questions about being poor. They had seemed so silly at the time. She knew from the bottom of her soul that Cora had lied when she said that Timothy had not been given time to choose. She was as sure of his love as she was sure of the love of God. She knew just how he would have answered his uncle. Throwing up his head and laughing at the thought of being dictated to over a thing which really mattered.

But Timothy's side was not the only one. There was hers. Had she any right to let him make this sacrifice? She knew what it was like to be poor. He had no idea. Could all the love that she would give make up in the end for the position he had lost? They said, "love didn't last." She didn't believe that. But quite likely later on other things mattered too. Suppose she failed him. Ought she, to be responsible for the risk?

Alice was, as usual, in the kitchen when Ann came in. "Hurry up, darling," she said. "I've made a fish pie and it's piping hot." There was no answer. She looked round. She gave a gasp. "Mercy, child, what's the matter?"

"It's nothing—I mean it's only—"

The strain of the mental torment she had been in was too much for her. She slid on the floor in a heap.

It happened Nurse was in the house. She had got home early. In no time she had brought Ann round and had her on the sofa in the sitting-room.

"Now," she said firmly. "What's up? Girls like you don't go fainting all over the place for nothing."

Ann, still feeling curiously detached and unfocused, shook her head.

"It's nothing you could help me over. I mean, there is something, but it's nothing to do with my health."

Nurse laughed.

"That's something." Then her voice grew gentle. "Having trouble with that young man of yours?"

At the mention of Timothy two tears rolled out from under her eyelids.

"In a way—" she hesitated. "There is a way you might help. I've got to go away. Do you know anybody in a town out of London. I mean a biggish town where they'd want beauty specialists?"

Nurse managed not to look startled.

"Going away are you?"

"I must. I haven't told Mum and Dad yet."

"They'll be terribly upset."

Ann nodded.

"I don't like to think what Bunny'll say. But I must go." Nurse was impressed by her voice.

"Well, if you must, I might help. My Mother lives near Bristol. She'd be glad to have you."

"Thank you." Ann rolled over and faced the wall. "I'll tell them after supper."

Ann, looking ghastly, sat in an armchair by the fire. Alfred and Alice sat side-by-side facing her.

"I don't think a marriage could be right with that behind it," Ann said. "It's so one-sided. Everything given up for me."

"I expect he thinks you're worth it." Alfred suggested.

She nodded.

"Yes. But I don't want it. Let him give me up and go back to his uncle. Maybe we'll find a way to get married without all this."

Alice leaned forward.

"But, darling, must you be so violent. Couldn't you see him and explain how you feel?"

Ann shook her head.

"No. You see, I love him. If I see him I could never say all this. I'd just marry him no matter what happened. That's why I've got to go."

Alice looked at Alfred. Her look said, "I see her point. I'm not sure she's not right."

He cleared his throat.

"We would never stand in the way of what you thought right. You know that. If you feel you must go we won't stop you. But I don't want you doing things in a rush you might be sorry for. Suppose you now went to stay with Nurse's mother. We could explain about your fainting. Mr. Pert might keep your job open."

Ann gave a vague acquiescent move.

"I don't mind about that as long as I go. You see, I'm going to write to his uncle and say I've gone. That'll make it easy for Timothy. I mean he won't have to make the first move."

Alice put her elbows on her knees and rested her face in her hands.

"Sir Timothy'll come here you know. What are we to say?"

"Nothing. I'll write to him of course. He'll know I'm not here. He'll try and get my address out of you."

Alfred grunted.

"If I read him right he's not going to be all that easy. If he's told his uncle he'd rather have you than the job then I reckon he knows what he's about."

Ann looked up.

"Now. But suppose later on he was out of work. You know what that's like."

Alfred's eyes looked inward. He saw over the years. The planning and interest of his business. He saw, too, how these last years had been. Waking in the mornings to blank days. Lying down at night with the knowledge of a blank awakening. No—he could never advise a man to turn down a good safe job.

"If he went back to his uncle would you come back?"

Ann's face fit.

"Do you think I'd stay away from home a minute longer than I need?" She jumped up and sat between them, an arm round each. "Don't you think I'm going to miss you all? You old sillies."

Bunny drummed with his fingers on the window. The rain ran down it in grey streaks. Bunny sighed heavily.

"Haven't you got anything to do?" asked Alice.

"Yes, lots. But I haven't felt like doing things now Ann's away."

Alice came over and rubbed his hair backwards.

"Silly boy. Well, if you've nothing you want to do for yourself you can do it for other people. If I fetch my box of envelopes will you cut the stamps off for the hospital?"

Bunny looked pleased.

"Um. I'd like that. I'll get your scissors."

Alice fetched her box and watched Bunny sit at the kitchen table with a happy, absorbed face, busy at his snipping.

"You be good. I've got a bit of machining to do in the other room."

Bunny hummed at his work. Quite a nice pile of stamps. He wondered what hospitals wanted them for. People said they were for stamp collections but he couldn't imagine anyone wanting to buy used English three-halfpenny stamps. Suddenly he stopped cutting. This envelope was in Ann's handwriting. He looked at it closely. Then suddenly he smiled. "Bristol." It said so on the postmark. Bristol was in

England anyway. He had been afraid she had gone a long way off. Somewhere as far as France.

The front door bell rang. He sat up straight and listened. He heard Timothy's voice. He bounced off his chair and ran down the passage.

"Sir Timothy, Sir Timothy!"

But it was not the Timothy he knew who stood there. It was a grey-faced man who took him gently by the shoulders and moved him to one side.

"Not now, old man. I've got to have a word with your mother and father."

Alice and Alfred were in the hall. Alice opened the sitting-room door.

"Come in here. We were expecting you."

Bunny slowly went back into the kitchen. It had seemed awful to him when Ann went away. But Ann just couldn't know what she had done to Sir Timothy. If she did she would come back at once.

Bunny was an honourable child, not the sort to listen at doors. But this seemed important. Above ordinary things like that. He crept along the passage and stood in the shadow outside the sitting-room.

"You know what she's written to me," said Timothy. "But here's what she sent to Uncle George."

Dear Sir,

I understand that because of me you are taking away Timothy's job. Well please give it back because I have gone. I've left London and he won't find me.

Yours faithfully,

Ann Lane.

"And across the bottom is written by my uncle: *'You had better come and see me about this.'*"

"She won't come back until you're working at Munster's," said Alice.

"But I can't go back there." Timothy's voice was strained. "You don't know my uncle. He won't change his mind."

"Neither will Ann," put in Alfred. "Not when she sees a thing is wrong."

There was silence, then Timothy said in a voice which sounded as if he were nearly crying, only of course Bunny knew grown-up men never did that:

"You mean you won't tell me where she is?"

"Yes," said Alice. She obviously was crying. She spoke in a sob.

Alfred was very gruff.

"I'm afraid so."

Bunny had only just time to step out of the way, for in one second Timothy was blundering down the passage and out through the front door.

Bunny looked after him. He felt so sorry for him it hurt. Why was everybody being so mean to him? He had always been so kind to them. Suddenly his face set in determined lines. Well, they could all be mean if they liked, but he wouldn't be. Timothy had been his friend and he'd be his friend back. He knew where he lived, and he had a penny which would help with the bus fare.

He daren't go upstairs to fetch his things for fear of being caught. Alice and Alfred were still in the sitting-room. He slipped into the kitchen. There was a penny he knew on the dresser, it wasn't his penny but he could put that straight when he got back. He crept along the passage. Very softly he opened the front door and slipped out into the drenching rain.

That walk to Hill Street was a nightmare. He never could walk far and the bus did not help as much as he had hoped. When you have a bad heart walking with rain blowing in your face makes things worse. Then he didn't know the way and people's directions seemed to make it more difficult to find. He wandered up and down at least six of the wrong streets. He got so tired he had to sit on a step a second or two to rest and then was cold and could not stop his teeth chattering. Then at last, when he had almost given up he saw it, "Hill Street." Somehow he found the number. Somebody took him up in a lift. He rang a bell.

It was not Timothy who answered.

"No. Sir Timothy's out. Is it a message?"

Bunny was just about at the end of his tether. He gripped the strange man convulsively.

"Yes. Say Ann's at—"

Then he collapsed.

"How is he?" asked Timothy.

He and Alfred were talking in the hospital corridor. Bunny was so bad they had put him in a small room on his own.

"Shocking," said Alfred. "Not got much chance really. Not pneumonia with his heart."

"Is Ann coming?"

"We tried to telegraph her last night. But it seems where Nurse's mother lives is outside somewhere. They said they couldn't deliver till the morning."

"Mercy, man, why didn't you get hold of me? I'd have got it to her."

"There seemed no chance to get away. We never left here all night."

"Is she on her way now?"

"That's the bad part. We've just had a telegram. She's gone out for a long day. They don't seem to know where." Alice came and found them. Her face seemed to Timothy to have sagged and aged half a lifetime since he last saw her. She looked at Alfred.

"He keeps asking for Ann. I don't like to tell him she's coming. I've never told him lies."

"She is coming," said Timothy. "I'll drive down and fetch her."

"You might miss her. She'll take the first train."

"All the same I can try and if I may I'll pop in and tell Bunny I'm off. He'll be pleased about that. After all, it was to send me to Bristol, poor kid, that he's like he is."

Bunny, very grey-skinned, was propped up by pillows. His breathing hurt to listen to. He was using all his energy for the almost hopeless business of keeping himself alive. But a faint expression of pleasure crossed his face a sight of Timothy.

"I've got something I want to ask you."

Timothy nodded. He turned to the nurse.

"Can I have a word with him alone?" He drew a chair next to the bed. "Well, what is it?"

"Do you think you could find Ann?"

"Yes. I'm just off. I'm bringing her back with me."

"Truly?"

"Truly. Unless she gets here before me."

Bunny tried to hold out his hand.

"Nobody's here, are they?"

"No."

"Well, I'll tell you something, only Mum and Dad mustn't know. I'm frightened. You see, when they brought me here they let Dad and Mum stay all night. That means I'm on the danger list." He gave a small scared whimper. "I don't want to die."

Timothy put a hand over one of his.

"Nor are you going to."

"I don't think I will if Ann's here. I'm never frightened then."

Timothy tightened his grip.

"Between now and somewhere tonight I'm bringing Ann along, and you've got to be here waiting. See? That's a promise. And as a matter of fact we'll be worth waiting for. I've got a big surprise for you."

"About Ann?"

"No, it's something for you." He got up. "Now, no more talk about dying. It's pure rot. You just be quiet here till I get back with Ann. Shan't be long."

Nurse's mother was an old dear and kindness itself and where she lived was pleasant. Spring had arrived and every tree was loaded with blossom, and every garden shimmering with daffodils. But Ann could not appreciate anything. She felt almost as if she were dead and seeing this world from another. The first days she wandered about, her eyes on everything, seeing nothing, answering with a polite "yes" or "no" when anybody spoke. Nurse's mother had been a nurse herself. She could not bear to see anyone in such a state.

"It's a kind of shock you have had, dear. You've screwed yourself up to come away and that's all you can do at present. You've used so much energy to get the courage to break away, you've none left. You've got to give nature a chance now to give you some more."

"Yes," Ann agreed.

"Now tomorrow if it's fine I don't want to see a sight of you. You'll take your lunch in a packet, and go out over Clifton Downs way! We'll see what a bit of wind and sun can do."

Ann was a Londoner. There had been no money for holidays these last years, though when she had been small there had been fortnights at Bognor or Folkestone. Those times at the sea had been mostly spent on the beach. She had never had a chance to wander alone with no plans.

That day on the downs was a revelation to her. She did not know the names of the birds she saw and heard. She did not know the names of most of the flowers she picked. She spent the morning idly wandering. Then when she was hungry she sat under a pussy willow and ate her sandwiches. Afterwards she stretched out on her back and stared at the blue of the sky, between the gold of the pussy willow heads.

It was then she began to come alive again. She did not feel better about Timothy. She still ached all over when she thought she might not see him again. But as she stretched flat on the downs she felt the hammer of Nature's heart suck the exhaustion out of her and strength flow in. And she knew forever that no matter what life might do to her, she had in her the courage not to break.

It was getting dark when she turned her face homeward. She paused just before she reached the road and raised her face to the sky.

"Please don't let him be too unhappy either."

Nurse's mother was on the doorstep.

"Come in dear. I've got a pot of tea on the table."

Ann stood on the mat unmoving.

"What is it? Something's the matter?"

"I've had a telegram. It came just after you left. It's your brother. He's ill, they want you back."

"Bunny!" Ann ran to the stairs. "Look up a train while I throw my things in my case."

"It's packed dear. And there's no need. The gentleman is motoring you up."

Ann turned.

"What gentleman?"

"I don't know. He came before dinnertime. He's been out looking for you ever since."

"Where is he now?"

"He'll be back. He went up to the bus stop to see if he could catch you. You get ready and put on your big coat. Then you can start the moment he comes."

Ann came down the stairs. Timothy was in the hall. He took the case from her. He put his arm round her.

"Come on, old lady."

Ann had asked and learned all there was to know about Bunny. Timothy was driving fast but the blackness ahead seemed to stretch forever.

"How soon will we be there?"

"From here if we're lucky we might make it in two and a half hours."

She looked at the clock.

"We've been ages already."

"I know. I daresay he's asleep."

She spoke under her breath.

"Or dead."

He did not answer. Her teeth began a nervous chatter. He said:

"There's another rug at the back."

"I'm not cold. Go on."

Quite suddenly he slowed down. They stopped at an inn.

"We'll stop here. You must have a drink."

"I don't want to stop. I want to get to Bunny."

He went into the inn alone. She sat champing with impatience. Presently he reappeared with a glass of hot milk.

"Drink that."

She smelt brandy.

"It's got brandy in it. I don't want it."

He seemed to lose his temper.

"Drink it and don't be a little fool. Five minutes won't affect Bunny, and you being ill, too, won't help anybody."

His tone was so rough it startled her. She drank the glass off without a word. Then got out of the car and went into the inn.

When they had started again he took her hand.

"I'm not really such a brute. But someone has got to be strong-minded."

She squeezed his hand.

"It would be too awful if you weren't here. I can't talk about us tonight."

"Of course not."

"You told me what's the matter with Bunny. But you didn't say what you thought. Has he got a chance?"

"Just a shred. I've an idea he'll hold on till you come. After that I don't know. I think if I were you I'd loll the old head on to my shoulder. A fashion set by a certain Sally, the bridesmaid. You might get a bit of sleep."

It was nearly eleven when they reached the hospital. Timothy rang the bell. In a low voice he told the porter who they were, and asked a question. Climbing the stairs he gave Ann's arm a squeeze.

"I told you he'd be alive to see you."

Bunny was just alive. All the will in him kept his eyes fixed on the door. He could not see very well. He could hardly hear. The effort to breathe clouded all other faculties.

Alice sat one side of the bed and Alfred the other. Timothy never forgot their faces. Alice's smile like a painted grin on a mask. Alfred's stony agonised look.

Ann seemed to see nobody but Bunny. She gave her mother a gentle touch and slipped into her chair.

"Bunny." There seemed a twitch in the corners of his mouth as if he recognised her. Then you could see him let go. All his effort of watching was rewarded. He gave up.

That set Ann fighting. He could not just slip off like that. She took his hands. She used every ounce of her will power.

"Bunny, Bunny. Listen."

Then she talked softly, she told him of her day. She lived it again and took him with her. The birds. The flowers. The pussy palm. Then she remembered the health that came back as she lay on the ground. She tried to pass that on. Let it throb down her arms, and through his feeble body. She willed strength to him with such violence that she was blind and deaf to everything else. Then, suddenly, as if a cord were cut between them she knew he had let go. She blinked her eyes and brought them back to focus. She saw his little grey face. The limp hand in hers. A sob rose in her throat.

A sister leaned over the bed. She looked at Bunny. Then she gently disengaged Ann's hand from his. She half lifted her off the chair. She led her out of the room.

"It was no good," sobbed Ann. "But I did try, and now he's dead."

"Dead!" The sister gave her a friendly squeeze.

"He's asleep, you silly girl."

"Well, if it isn't my best man."

Timothy swung round.

"Mona! Did you have a lovely honeymoon with that poisonous man you married?"

"I did." Mona laid her hand on his arm. "If you'll move into the light a bit I'll get a better view of your face."

They were both leaving Harrods. It was a wet and gloomy morning. Mona eyed him thoughtfully.

"How my boyfriends do go to pieces when I'm away. What the Hell have you been doing? You look like warmed-up death. And why are you strolling around in the morning, instead of making soap?"

He took her arm.

"Come along and have a cocktail and you shall hear the frightful tale."

They went to the Park Lane. Over a drink Mona heard it all. Watching his face as he talked of the Lanes, of Bunny's illness, and mostly of Ann, she dropped all her flippancy. This was serious. This was something too real to laugh about. Love affairs were not funny when they went as badly as this.

"And do you mean," she said at last, "she won't see you."

"That's right. I run into her sometimes visiting the kid. But she won't be engaged. She says I've got to go back to Munster's."

"And can't you?"

"It's no good. I saw Uncle George after Ann wrote to him. He says my place is still there if I give her up."

"A deadlock."

"Absolutely."

"What's Ann doing?"

Timothy passed her a cigarette.

"She's back at Pertinax. She was only away those few days."

Mona smoked thoughtfully in silence.

"There must be a way out. If only I could see it." Timothy snapped his lighter shut.

"The only way I know is for the old man to see her. I think he'd fall for her. But I can't work it."

Mona's face lit up.

"Of course. That's the right idea. I know what we'll do. We'll stage it."

"How?"

She held up her hand to stop him.

"Ssh. Don't interrupt. I'm thinking."

Half an hour later, Mona walked in at the door of Maison Pertinax. Lila, all smiles, came forward. Mona nodded a good morning.

"Where's Mr. Pert?"

Lila looked slightly surprised. But it was not her place to argue with the customers. She pressed Mr. Pert's bell.

Mr. Pert was delighted to see Mona. She was the daughter of one of his oldest customers. She was the sort he loved to serve.

"I'm not a bit interested in my face and hair today," she explained. "As a matter of fact I've come to ask a favour."

Mr. Pert bowed.

"I'm sure it'll be a pleasure to grant, m'lady."

"Could you spare Ann Lane to come out to lunch with me?"

Lila's eyes goggled. Could she have heard right?

Mr. Pert was surprised and slightly shocked. In his philosophy such as Mona did not mix with such as his young ladies, but he showed no sign of what he felt. He turned to Lila.

"Is Miss Lane serving a customer, Miss Grey?"

Lila, with a sickening feeling of impotence, knew Ann just to have finished a customer. She felt she simply could not bear it if Ann of all people was allowed out early and with Lady Mona. It would be unbearable.

Iris, running along the passage, had heard Mona's request. In passing she looked in on Connie, ostensibly to borrow some curling tongs, actually to give her the signal to keep her ears skinned. Something worthwhile was happening outside.

Betty was manicuring June's customer. June's cubicle was nearest the desk. Betty and June exchanged a glance.

"I think you need another few minutes under the drier, Madam," said June, hurriedly covering her customer's head. She slipped up the passage to Agnes.

Agnes was not working, she was gossiping with Biddy. Both girls moved quietly down the corridor within earshot.

"Poor Kitty," Biddy whispered. "Wish she could listen, but she's doing a bleach."

Lila was pretending to look through the engagement book.

"Well—" she said, playing for time.

Mr. Pert was annoyed. Lady Mona was not the sort of person he kept waiting.

"Please hurry, Miss Grey. Is Miss Lane serving a customer, or isn't she?"

June goggled over the drier at Betty. Betty was so excited she dug the orange-stick into her customer, who let out an annoyed yelp.

Iris came into Connie's cubicle again.

"Can I take that now?" she asked, picking up an imaginary object from behind the customer's back and at the same time giving Connie a triumphant dig.

Agnes and Biddy clung together.

"She's being told where she gets off at last," Biddy whispered ecstatically.

Lila fumbled with the appointment book.

"Not at the moment," she said, unwillingly. "But one is expected."

"Well, well, well," said Mr. Pert crossly. "I daresay Miss Briggs will take her. Go along at once and arrange it."

"It's too good to be true," breathed Biddy.

Lila, quite white with passion, came to Ann.

"Lady Mona is here. She wishes to see you." She went straight out. It was no good her seeing Minnie Briggs. The expected customer was hers, anyway.

Every eye that could reasonably leave its work was taking a peep when Ann met Mona.

"Hullo, duckie," said Mona, giving her a kiss. "Mr. Pert says you can lunch with me, so get on your things."

Spellbound, everybody watched Mona and Ann walk out. Mr. Pert went back to his office.

"It's ridiculous," said Lila to Minnie Briggs, who had come to look for her customer. "Lady Mona seems to forget who she is."

Mr. Pert had not shut his door. Lila's voice reached him. What she said touched his most vulnerable spot. In his esteem, Lady Mona and her class could do no wrong. Certainly shop assistants such as Lila could not criticise them. White with rage he came back to the desk.

"Miss Grey, you go too far. Please don't forget yourself."

The girls could hardly wait for lunch. As each finished she raced to the basement. Pleasure in the defeat of their enemy made their voices ring. The noise grew deafening.

"Girls!" Lila came to the top of the stairs. "What are you thinking of? Don't you know we still have two custom-ers here?"

Iris stood at the bottom of the stairs.

"I'm sorry, Miss Grey, us girls go too far. We forget ourselves."

What Lila answered was drowned in a howl of laughter.

Mona drove Ann back to her flat.

"We'd better be alone," she said. "Because I'm full of schemes and you've got to hear them."

Over lunch they talked of the honeymoon and the wedding. Afterwards Mona led the way to her own sitting-room.

"Now," she said, "I've seen Timothy this morning. He looks like warmed-up death."

"I know. All the same, I believe I'm right. I can't have him giving up everything for me. It's all right now, but what about later on?"

"Timothy says it's no good arguing with you. I expect he knows. But I've an idea. You know Timothy's Uncle George is an awful snob. His idea of heaven is a house full of dukes."

"That's why he can't stand the thought of me."

"I know. He just sees you with the shop background. Now suppose he met you on a ducal background."

"How could he?"

"My godmother is a duchess, and the biggest pet that ever breathed. We'll make her give a party, she'll invite you, and sitting next to you will be Uncle George. After that it's up to you."

"You mean if he met me like that he mightn't mind me?" Mona laughed.

"I suspect however he met you he wouldn't mind you. The trouble is he's never seen you."

"Would a green evening frock be all right for a party like that? It's one the models had worn that I bought through a girl at Bertna's."

"Any dress of Bertna's is always right. But for something like this we'll dress you up. New clothes do give a girl confidence."

Bunny lay on the sofa, his white face faintly fit by a flush of excitement. Alice and Alfred stood against the wall. Ann turned slowly round. She had on a frock of parchment-coloured faille. It was stiffened and was as bouffant and feminine as anything worn by our grandmothers. Round her neck and on her wrist were pearls. On the side of her head was a gardenia. Lying over a chair was Mona's ermine cape.

"Gosh!" said Bunny.

Alfred nodded appraisingly.

"You've nothing to worry about. You look every inch a duchess yourself."

Alice smiled.

"But she is one. Didn't you know. When the stork was bringing my baby along he had another one to deliver on the same trip, and he made a mistake. The Lady Honora Vere de Vere came bumping down our chimney. And Miss Ann Lane fell clattering into the duke's kitchen."

Bunny laughed.

"Go on Mum. Finish that one."

Alice shook her head.

"No, maybe Ann can take over the story-telling. She might know the end of it in the morning. Come on, young man. It's time we carried you up to bed."

"Just a minute, Mum. I want to ask Ann something, it's a secret."

"All right," Alice put her arm through Alfred's. "Outside for us. We're used to being ordered about."

"What is it, darling?" said Ann.

Bunny rested on his elbow.

"When I was so ill Timothy told me he had a surprise for me. When I was better he told me what it was; only you were the only person who could make it happen."

"What is it?"

"I mustn't say, and you wouldn't see him, so he couldn't ask you. But tonight he's going to—at least he is, if he can."

"Is it something you want dreadfully?"

"Yes."

She kissed him.

"All right then, don't fuss, if I can make it happen, it will."

"Do you look a gorgeous beast?" said Timothy.

"Oh dear." Ann put her hand in his. "I'm so scared, my knees are knocking together."

"You. A woman who dares to slap mud on to the faces of half London to be afraid to eat dinner next to my Uncle George."

"I can't help it," Ann whispered. "I am. It's so terribly important."

Mona had made her plans well. The butler was ordered not to announce Ann by name. Sir George, eyeing the menu card, wondered who he was next to. He asked the woman on his other side.

"Who's the girl on my right?"

She had been trained in her part.

"That? I forget her name. A great friend of Mona's."

"Nice lookin' girl," said George. "Nice look of breedin'." He turned to Ann.

Ann, more in desperation than by design discussed soap. Soap seemed a suitable subject for Sir George and nobody knew more about its washing abilities than she did. She knew hair soaps and soap flakes intimately. Sir George was charmed. It was inconceivable that so much beauty could be allied to such intelligence.

After dinner when the party were breaking up into groups for bridge and roulette, he sought the duchess.

"Who was that charmin' girl on my right at dinner?"

The Duchess paused while she looked round and caught Mona's eye. It was a triumphant "we've hooked him now" look.

"That! Surely you know. One of the most delightful girls. Miss Ann Lane."

Timothy was talking to Ann. Sir George came across to them. He laid a hand on his shoulder.

"I think, my dear," he said to Ann, "I've done you an injustice. Gettin' a bit old fashioned I'm afraid. Ought to have guessed from your letter you were the right sort of girl. I expect all this is a lot of poppycock. I daresay they've got you here to fool me. Well, they haven't. I like you as a person, not because I meet you dinin' with a duchess, and I'm hopin' to like you as a niece."

*

"You must stop kissing me," said Ann. "Even if we are engaged, I'm sure the chauffeur can see."

Timothy held her closer.

"Who cares?" After a pause he said, "Listen, my sweet, I've been wanting to talk over a plan with you. Only you wouldn't see me."

She laid her cheek on his shoulder.

"I have missed you."

"I'm afraid I'm going to say something a bit gloomy, but I believe in fairy things. Old Bunny isn't a good life. Nobody knows how he got through the illness. He wouldn't stand up to another."

She sat up with a jerk.

"He's got to. He likes being alive, even if he is always ill."

"As I see things the best chance he'd have would be to live in the country. I've been nosing around. I've got just the place."

"Mum and Dad couldn't afford it."

"Good air," Timothy went on unmoved by her interruptions. "Got a nice garden. It's off the main road, but it's easy to get around in a car."

She faced him.

"Are you trying to give this to Mum and Dad? You know they wouldn't take it."

"No, Sally-Ann, I'm hoping you'll like it as an engagement present. And I'm hoping that your superb tact, which you've used so well on Uncle George, you'll make them take it from you."

"This is the secret Bunny said you were going to tell me."

"Yes."

"And I'm the only person who can make it happen?"

"That's right."

She lay back.

"It would be nice," said Timothy, "if while you were thinking you put your cheek back on my shoulder. It was very pleasant having it there."

Ann snuggled against him.

"It's not big, is it?"

"No. A cottage on our old place, as a matter of fact."

"Near where Cora lives?" He nodded. "She's going to be mad about us."

He held her close.

"I suspect she's got a good deal on her conscience. We needn't fuss about her."

"I do, though. She loves you. It must be awful not to be going to marry you."

They were silent a moment. Then Ann laughed.

"Did you say there was a car?"

"Yes, just a small thing. Must have something to get around in."

"You remember the first night we met? My frock was new, and Mum said when she saw me that I was a fairy. They all had a wish. Mum wished for a car, and Bunny for a house in the country with a garden. One of Mum's fairy tales is coming true."

"What did your father wish for?"

"He said he didn't want me going so far away he couldn't get at me."

"He'll get his, too."

"I'm not sure he meant just living near."

Timothy smiled. He held her close.

"I'm quite sure he didn't, Sally-Ann."

CHAPTER TWELVE

ANN turned over, and from force of habit picked up the alarum clock. From force of habit, too, she held it over her head, as she had done in the old days when she worked at Maison Pertinax. The discomfort of the position made her, as usual, open her eyes, and at once she laughed and put the clock down. It was seven o'clock and no alarum had woken her, it was just excitement, because today was the day. She went to the window and looked into the street. It was going to be fine. A little heat haze hung over the buildings, there was not a cloud in the sky, and there was that indescribable smell of London getting ready to endure a hot day. Ann hung out and looked at all the familiar sights, the dustbins, and the milk bottles, the black cat from over the way, the repulsive pink curtains of the house opposite; how queer that after today she would never see any of this again. She might, of course, pass this way, but it would be a different Ann, not the Ann that hustled out to work in all weathers, and tried to give a helping hand with the lodgers, but an Ann married to Timothy.

The thought of becoming this very day Lady Munster, gave Ann a curious feeling inside. It was not exactly fright, she couldn't be frightened of marrying Timothy, but a sort of quick snatching at what was left of her childhood. What would it be like to belong to somebody else? She curled back again in bed and pulled the sheets up to her chin. It was a good thing that Timothy was marrying a wife of her sort, people like him and Sir George meant to be nice and do the right thing, but only a girl who had worked herself really knew what girls who worked needed. She had been all over the Munster factory; she had seen the rest rooms and the Welfare Supervisor, and the sports grounds, and all the other expensive contrivances for keeping workers well and happy. She hadn't said anything at the time, she didn't suppose that she could coerce Timothy into anything, and she was quite certain that she would have no influence on Sir George; but there were ways. Perhaps she could let them think that they had thought of improvements themselves. The better accommodation for clothes, with lockups, so that if you had a date with anybody you had somewhere to keep your things, perhaps somewhere where you could change comfortably. Then the holiday system was very arbitrary. It was all very well giving some of them August and some of them September, and so on, it would probably work out all right if they all chose their own time, no harm in trying it, anyway. And then—At that point she stopped thinking of the Munster factory, today was her wedding day, time for factories later on. She thought about her wedding dress. How difficult it had been to be tactful with everyone. Dad, bless his heart, so touchy at any suggestion that he shouldn't pay for everything, as if he could, poor sweet, besides, there was Timothy to think of, all his relations, it would be a mistake for his sake to start them nudging and talking about King Cophetua and the beggar maid. How grand Mum had been, how lucky she was to have a mother that understood everything without having to be told. It was she who had suggested that a perfect dress that was not new, was better than something new off the peg. It was a piece of luck that Lady Mona chose parchment colour at the party when she had met Sir George. It had not been difficult to persuade her to let it go back to the dressmakers and have some sleeves put in. Lady Mona had wanted to buy her a new frock, she couldn't see that somebody else giving a new frock would hurt Dad, but she had given way and there was the faille frock hanging in the cupboard with long, tight sleeves and something clever done to fill in the neck.

Of course, it was really the veil and the head-dress and the train that would make the get-up, even Dad could not mind those being borrowed, for brides often borrowed accessories. It was a piece of luck, though, that they had no small relations that ought to be pages or bridesmaids, even children's clothes cost a lot. Far better to have Timothy's little cousins, to whom money meant nothing.

It had been a bit of a job about the reception. Funny old Dad to want to have it here; how Mum had laughed.

"This house was a bit off, old dear," she had said to him, "before we began to pack to move to the country, but now we've nothing to offer the guests but packing cases to sit on."

"I don't like Ann's reception being in a hotel and being paid for by the bridegroom," Alfred had argued. Alice had sat down at the table.

"All right, Mr. Proud, let's pay for our own guests. There's you and me and Bunny, and your brother, and the three Smith cousins, and the four lodgers and Nurse's mother, all the girls from Maison Pertinax and Mr. Pert, and a few more that I can't remember. You send the list in to Timothy and ask him what Claridge's are charging a head, and say we would like to pay for our lot."

Of course, Dad hadn't insulted Timothy by doing that; that was just Mum's cleverness. All the same, she had a nasty feeling that amongst all the happiness in the house; Mum singing as she packed, at the thought of a cottage in the country; Bunny heaps better already at the idea of a move, and her own radiance, that Dad alone felt a bit bruised inside. It was like that day when she had worn her green evening dress for the first time, and Mum had said she was a fairy and could give them each a wish and his wish had been, "I don't want you going so far away that we can't get at you." At the time she had not understood and had asked what he had meant, and he had said, "there's other ways of going away than travelling," even then she had not understood, but she did now. But he was wrong, utterly, hopelessly wrong, and all her life she would prove it. Being Lady Munster and being rich and things like that wouldn't matter at all. The Ann that had been born at 95 Anchor Street, Chelsea, was something that change of surroundings could not kill, and if ever she found herself feeling grand and forgetting, she would know it by the look in Dad's eyes.

Thinking so much made her wish it was time for breakfast, a cup of tea, she thought, would go down very well, and it would be rather fun to call Dad and Mum with a cup of tea for the last time. The last thing Mum had said when she went up to bed was that she was to stop in bed and not to move for anyone, that was all rubbish. How could a girl who woke at seven be expected to he still on her wedding morning?

"My, my, my, if it isn't the bride," said Nurse.

Ann was just in the mood for company and beamed at the sight of her boiling a kettle.

"I woke early and I thought I would like a cup of tea, and I thought I would take one up to Mum and Dad. Have you taken the milk in?"

Nurse caught hold of her arm.

"I haven't, but I will, m'lady."

Ann giggled and went to the back door.

"Doesn't it sound silly?"

Nurse fetched the teapot and poured in some water to heat it.

"My old lady doesn't think so. You've never known such a change in anyone. When she found that I lived in the same house as you did it was as if you'd given her a dose of monkey glands. Sitting up in bed, she was. What were you like? Where did you meet him? What were you going to wear for the wedding? What I didn't know I made up, it doesn't do you any harm and does me a lot of good. Going on the way we are she'll leave me a bit in her will."

Ann sat on the table.

"Funny, the interest people take in other people's lives. All these reporters want to write to the papers about me. I don't see how it can interest people to read in the papers about somebody they've never met."

Nurse tipped the drop of water out of the teapot and opened the tea canister.

"Don't talk so stupidly, old dear. People say it's love that makes the world go round. If you ask me, it's hope. What do all the girls think when they read about you? Not 'I wonder what she's like,' but 'if she's done it so might I.' What makes people interested in film stars? Most of them came from somewhere near the bottom like the rest of us, and look where they've got to. If you read of a duchess throwing the money about the way the film stars do, you'd say the world was unjust, and some people had all the luck. But when it's one of us spending millions we get a kick. One of us got to the top and making the kind of fool of themselves we'd all like to make of ourselves."

Ann watched her spoon the tea into the pot.

"You won't believe it, but in lots of ways I wish Timothy wasn't a baronet and wasn't rich."

Nurse turned to the gas stove and poured some boiling water into the pot. Her voice was a bit muffled.

"I do believe it, and it's because you're that kind of an old silly that all of us in this house are going into mourning. I've always said you were better than a daily dozen."

Ann slid off the table, and pulled her round to face her.

"You're not crying, are you, on my wedding morning?"

Nurse sniffed.

"And not ashamed either. I shan't be the first one to cry at a wedding." She put down the teapot. "Though mind you,

I shall try not to. Yellow isn't exactly my colour, but the hat was so smart at the price that I had to buy it. So as it's the first and last time in my fife I'm asked to a smart wedding I'll try and keep bright. Tears and a red nose spoil the picture."

Alfred and Alice were awake. Alice screamed at the sight of Ann.

"You naughty girl, what did I tell you?"

Ann put down the tray beside them and curled up on the end of the bed.

"I was awake, and I had a feeling I could do with some tea myself."

Alice took up the teapot and poured out a cup.

"Puts me in mind of my own wedding day. I couldn't sleep for excitement. Then I was worried about my dress." Ann smiled.

"I know, because it wasn't big enough in front?"

Alice nodded and passed her a cup of tea.

"That was when I put the stuffing in. Girls fancied curves at that time. My mother had let me have a bit more curve than I'd got, but I didn't think it was enough."

Ann chuckled.

"Funny, you sewing a pair of stockings into the front of you, and me trying not to have a bulge anywhere."

Alfred took his cup of tea from Alice.

"You may laugh, young woman, but your mother made a lovely bride."

Ann grinned at her mother.

"I've seen the photographs!"

"All this getting up early," said Alice, "doesn't mean you're getting up for breakfast."

"Not up," Ann agreed, "I'm putting on a dressing gown and having it with Bunny, but I'm fetching the tray."

"No you're not," Alice sipped her tea. "It's the last chance I've got of spoiling you, and you're not going to take it from me."

Ann leaned back against the bedrail.

"Last chance nothing. Some day I'll be having babies, I don't see me having them without you about. You can spoil me then."

Nobody said anything for a minute. Ann looked over her cup at the sunshine outside. Alice had a vision of the sort of nursery that she had always wanted for Ann and Bunny, and had a pleasurable throb at the thought that such a nursery could now come true.

Alfred felt a warmth inside which did not come from the tea. Ann might be making a grand marriage, but it was not changing her. She was still the Ann he loved.

By eleven, 95 Anchor Street, was in a seething state of excitement. Thomas Bloom stood on a chair and slowly pivoted in front of his mirror. It was a little mirror and he could not see all of himself at once, at the moment it was his legs he was examining. He had hired a morning suit and was studying the striped trousers. Thomas Bloom had never in his life worn a morning suit and could ill afford the guineas it had cost to hire one, and the thought of appearing in such an outfit filled him with agonising embarrassment. But he knew something about weddings, knew that one side of the aisle was reserved for the bride's friends, and the other for the bridegroom's. It had been a vivid picture of what Ann's side might look like that had made him take those hard saved guineas from the bank and visit Moss Brothers. One, at least, of her friends should do her credit.

Maggie Dean had a day off from School and had locked her door. Behind it she put a kettle on her gas ring. Out of the back of the cupboard she took a carefully hidden package. From her shelf she took a bowl. She had spent three times as much as she had ever spent before on a hat. If a mudpack could do even a tenth of what it claimed, then she was satisfied. That shiny black straw, with its red roses would have a proper setting.

"Oy! Mrs. La-ane. Mrs. La-ane."

Alice came to the door of her bedroom.

"What is it, Mr. Perkins?"

"Have you got a pair of scissors?"

"What sort?"

Oswald leaned over the banisters.

"I've got my blue suit back from the cleaners and it's looking a bit of all right, but now I've found there's a bit of fray round the cuffs of my best shirt, which could stand pruning."

Alice laughed.

"My basket's on the kitchen dresser. Take the scissors out of there and mind you put them back."

Alice went back into the bedroom and closed the door. Out of the cupboard she took her wedding garment. It was not new, it was last year's. It had been grey, now it was dyed rust colour, with it she had a rust-red hat. She made a face at it. "Not up to much for the bride's mother," she thought regretfully, then she gave herself a metaphorical punch in the ribs. "Anyway, who's going to look at you, and if we can't afford a new dress we can't."

"Mu-um."

Alice went to the door again.

"What is it, Bun?"

"Can you come to my room a minute?"

"Half a second, son." Bunny slept now in what had been the sitting-room, for it saved the stairs. Alice went down to him. "What is it, old man?"

Alfred was in the room and so was Ann. Bunny's voice was shrill with excitement.

"Shut your eyes, Mum." Alice obediently shut them. "Now open."

Every woman has her idea of what a dress should be, even if she knows such a one will never come her way. Alice had always thought that a bride's mother at a wedding should wear blue. Not a harsh blue, but a blue with a bit of the Mediterranean in it, and somewhere about it, because it was a colour she loved, petunia. Once, some time before telling one of her fairy tales to Ann and Bunny, she had described herself in such a dress, now when she opened her eyes it was lying on the bed in front of her. And not only a dress but a blue hat to match, with a petunia trimming, and beside them in a box a bouquet of carnations. Alice looked at Ann, startled.

"Darling, you shouldn't. You know Dad and I wouldn't want you to spend any money on us."

Bunny bounced up and down on the bed.

"It wasn't Ann. It wasn't. It was Dad."

Alice turned to Alfred, her eyes misted with tears.

"Alfred, you never did. You know we haven't the money."

Alfred looked sheepish.

"I had a bit put away. It was left over from 'Ann Investments, Ltd.' I had kept it to get Ann something for her wedding. She knew about it, so she and I, we thought perhaps this would be a good way to spend it."

Alice looked at the clothes with tears pouring down her cheeks.

"Silly, aren't I. But I was so ashamed of sitting in the front row in my old brown."

"Don't cry, Mum," wailed Ann, "or I shall cry too."

That pulled Alice together.

"No you don't. I'm not going to have you looking puffy on your wedding day." She held out her hand. "You come up to my room and help me to put it on."

Timothy sent cars for everybody. In the first went the four boarders. In the second Bunny was carefully lifted in his wheeled chair and with him went Alice. Alfred and Ann had strict injunctions not to get into their car until twenty minutes to two.

"Oh dear," said Ann. "It's like waiting at the dentist's, Dad."

Alfred felt in his pocket and took out a little jewel box.

"Timothy said I was to give you this, it would make you laugh."

Ann opened the box. Inside was a little ring, worn, and old-fashioned. She took it to the window and turned it to the light.

"What a funny old thing. Oh, look! There's something written inside it. Listen, it's what a great-grandmother said, 'a sweetness as of honey.'" She put it on her little finger and came to her father and took his hand. "But it doesn't make me want to laugh a bit."

The organ swelled into "Praise My Soul the King of Heaven." Alfred and Ann came slowly up the aisle. The heads of the crowded church turned to look.

"S'truth," said Iris to Connie. "I'd praise my soul, too, if I was her."

Connie gave her an angry nudge.

"Shut up. Try and pretend you've been in a church before even if you haven't."

"Ah, sure," said Norah to June. "There's the glorious soul of her, shining out like the sun over Connemara."

"Funny," June sighed. "She's never done a thing about it, and look what she looks like, and me going to the League every night and not a bit off."

Agnes stared at them severely over her glasses.

"Ssh. This may be a wedding, but it's a church all the same."

"What are you crying for?" Biddy whispered to Kitty. "You're marrying your Tom next week."

"That's why," Kitty sniffed. "I'd never have married him but for her. Fancy, with all she's got to think about, her remembering me and Tom and getting Sir Timothy to park that old mother of his."

Mr. Pert, very dapper in what had been the latest thing in morning suits in the years before the Great War, looked at Ann with pained surprise.

"Beautiful. And couldn't appear more of a lady if she was born to it. I don't know what things are coming to."

Ann was quite unconscious of the staring eyes. She was even unconscious of Alfred's trembling arm. Ahead of her lay Timothy and ahead of them both lay life together. Her heart was so full of happiness her feet scarcely seemed to move, she felt drawn to him, as if he were a magnet.

"—to have and to hold from this day forward for better for worse, for richer for poorer, in sickness and in health, to love, cherish, and to obey, until death do us part—"

Alfred looked at Alice out of the corner of his eye. They said nothing, but she smiled. She knew exactly what he was thinking. With them it had been "for poorer," with Ann it would be "for richer," but would she be happier? A wordless "she couldn't be" passed between them.

Receptions are confusing for the bride. Ann felt her face had been kissed off. Minnie Briggs, when she reached her in the queue, looked at her anxiously.

"The make-up I gave you has held up well, but a few more kisses and you'll be through."

"Take off your gloves presently, allanah," whispered Norah. "Sure and I put so much love into polishing your nails it's a shame for no one to see them."

The girls had tossed up who should do Ann's hair and Iris had won. She looked at Ann critically.

"When I think of the time I spent fiddling with your curls and the time you must have spent hiding it all out of sight under your veil I could be sick." Then she gave Ann's hand a squeeze. "All the same, you look a peach. Do us girls credit."

It seemed no time to Ann before she was in a bedroom in the hotel, being changed, and scarcely a minute later before she was in the hall saying goodbye.

"Goodbye."

"Good luck."

"God bless you."

The last kisses were for her family.

"Goodbye, Mum, and don't get too tired with the move. Goodbye, Dad, I expect to see that garden a show by the time I come back." She knelt by Bunny's chair. "Goodbye, darling. I'll send you a postcard every single day."

In the car on the way to Croydon Aerodrome Timothy pulled Ann into his arms, gently he laid her head on his shoulder. They drove like that for quite a while before he whispered.

"Comfortable, Lady Munster?"

She gave a contented wriggle.

"Perfectly, thank you, Sir Timothy."

THE END

FURROWED MIDDLEBROW

*titles available in paperback only

**pseudonym of Noel Streatfeild

www.ingramcontent.com/pod-product-compliance
Lightning Source LLC
Chambersburg PA
CBHW030756190726
48285CB00003B/886